double dutch

SHARON M. DRAPER

ALADDIN PAPERBACKS
New York London Toronto Sydney

For my brother, Jeffrey

Many thanks to all of the dynamic jumpers on the Cincinnati
Double Dutch teams, and to all the participants in the
World Championships. You are all champions!
For more information about how to start a
Double Dutch team in your community,
please write to:
The American Double Dutch League
4220 Eads Street, N.E.
Washington, D.C. 20019
1-800-982-ADDL
www.addl.org

This book is a work of fiction. Any references to historical events, real people, or real locales
are used fictitiously. Other names, characters, places, and incidents are the product of the
author's imagination, and any resemblance to actual events or locales or persons, living or
dead, is entirely coincidental.

First Aladdin Paperbacks edition January 2004
Text copyright © 2002 by Sharon Draper

ALADDIN PAPERBACKS
An imprint of Simon & Schuster
Children's Publishing Division
1230 Avenue of the Americas
New York, NY 10020

Also available in an Atheneum Books for Young Readers hardcover edition.
Designed by O'Lanso Gabbidon
The text of this book was set in Baskerville.
Manufactured in the United States of America
16   18   20   19   17   15

The Library of Congress has cataloged the hardcover edition as follows:
Draper, Sharon M. (Sharon Mills)
Double Dutch / by Sharon M. Draper.
p. cm.
Summary: Three eighth-grade friends, preparing for the International Double Dutch
Championship jump rope competition in their hometown of Cincinnati, Ohio, cope with
Randy's missing father, and Yo Yo's encounter with the class bullies, and a secret Delia is too
embarrassed to share.
ISBN-13: 978-0-689-84230-6 ISBN-10: 0-689-84230-9 (hc.)
[1. Rope skipping—Fiction. 2. Contests—Fiction. 3. Dyslexia—Fiction. 4. Friendship—Fiction.
5. Schools—Fiction. 6. Afro-Americans—Fiction. 7. Cincinnati (Ohio)—Fiction.] I. Title.
PZ7.D78325 Do 2002
[Fic]—dc21 00-050247
ISBN-13: 978-0-689-84231-3 ISBN-10: 0-689-84231-7 (pbk.)

one

"LOOK OUT, GIRL, HERE COME THE TOLLIVER TWINS! Have mercy! They look like they're ready to bite something." Delia pulled her books close to her body and tried to avoid what looked like was going to be a direct confrontation with the two most feared boys at the school—Tabu and Titan Tolliver.

"Or kill something," Charlene whispered, eyes wide with real concern. "I wouldn't want to be alone in a room with them. Every time they pass me, I get so scared, I feel like I'm gonna wet my pants!"

"That's disgusting!" Delia said, laughing, as she glanced at Charlene.

"I ain't lyin'! I'm scared for real! I heard they kill puppies and kittens for fun. Felicity Johnson lives next door to them, and she told me she found her kitten dead on her front steps. It had been stabbed with a knife," Charlene said dramatically, shuddering at the thought.

"I heard that, too. But that's no proof that the twins killed her kitten," Delia said, trying to sound reasonable. "Sometimes kids just make that stuff up 'cause it sounds gross."

"Greg Mason's dog was also killed. Stabbed. And he lives down the street from the Tollivers," Charlene added with authority. "His next-door neighbor's cousin told me."

"I heard Greg's dog got hit by a car," Delia replied. But she still watched nervously as the two unsmiling boys approached them. It was as if a double shadow was heading their way.

"The dog is still dead," Charlene said, refusing to accept any other explanation. "And Greg's house is awfully close to the Tollivers'. Yo Yo told me the twins carry knives and sawed-off shotguns and hand grenades in their book bag." Charlene spoke as if she believed it. "You believe that?" Charlene asked, hoping Delia would say no.

"Most times I don't believe Yolanda, but those two are some scary dudes. I wouldn't be surprised at anything. Before you know it, we'll be needing metal detectors on the front doors around here."

"I'm surprised they haven't got around to that—makin' this place feel like a prison. Most of the big-city schools have all kinds of security these days," Charlene stated with authority.

"Yeah, I know. Small-town schools, too. It's a shame. Why do you think the Tollivers dress in the same black clothes every day?" Delia asked in a whisper. "You think that's all the clothes they have?"

"Maybe they want to show people how bad they are!" Charlene said softly.

"They made me a believer!"

"You got that right! Quit whispering! They know we're talkin' about them!" Delia and Charlene tried to move out of the way of the twins, but the halls were crowded, and everybody seemed to be trying to do the same thing.

Titan and Tabu—tall and impressive-looking, dressed

exactly alike in black jeans, black sweaters, and black skullcaps—strode through the hall not as two people but as one unified force. Their faces wore the same menacing frown, their fists were clenched into the same tight threat, and their thick black boots stomped in unison on the scuffed hallway floor. They carried no books, even though it was almost third bell. They glared at Charlene and Delia as they pushed through the crowded hallway. With his shoulder, Titan pushed Delia against the lockers, and Tabu knocked Charlene out of the way in the other direction as they passed. She lost her balance and fell to the floor in a heap of books and papers. Tabu and Titan glanced back at them as though to make sure their authority had terrified the two girls. It had. Delia said nothing and looked the other way rather than risk a confrontation. A sea of people in the hall separated as the two forged a path through the crowd.

"Kids treat Tabu and Titan like they're Moses in the wilderness," Charlene said with disgust as she picked up her books and papers. "Looks like the parting of the waters of the Red Sea as they go through there."

"No, not Moses," Delia said, rubbing her shoulder. "Moses was a holy man. Those two are . . . bad. I can feel it."

"They give me chills. They don't talk to people, they don't speak up in class—I think some of the teachers are scared of them too," Charlene declared as they headed on to their classes.

Delia sighed. "Miss Benson, my English teacher, is real scared of them, I know. She's just a first-year teacher—she doesn't know how to handle the rough kids yet. It's all she can do to figure out how to handle the thirty-one other kids in the class, let alone the Terrible Tollivers. There's the bell. That's where I'm headed now. Wish me luck."

"Peace out, Delia. Stay clear of those two."

"You don't have to warn me. Besides, I got enough problems of my own to take time to worry about them. Later."

Delia hurried down the hall and into her classroom just before Miss Benson closed the door. She was glad her seat was in the front of the room, far away from Tabu and Titan, who sat in the very last row in the back. Miss Benson had not tried to change their seats when they transferred into the class during the second week of school. Delia figured the teacher wanted to keep as much space as possible between her and those two openly hostile boys.

Miss Benson was very young—just out of college. She still had hints of teenage acne on her face and she dressed more like a teenager than a teacher. Delia had thought she looked really uncomfortable in the business suit that she had worn for Open House—she was probably a jeans-and-sweatshirt kind of person. She liked to play with her hair, and she giggled sometimes when she should have put on a stony face. But Delia liked her because Miss Benson was energetic and excited about teaching, not like many of her other teachers, who seemed so tired every day. Delia also liked her because she could fool Miss Benson so easily. Miss Benson still had much to learn.

Delia forgot about Tabu and Titan for the moment as class began.

Miss Benson tried to be pleasant and conversational as she took attendance. "Quentin Bates? Glad to see you back. That flu bug is a doozy! Make sure you see me after class for makeup work."

Quentin coughed and nodded.

"Delia Douglas?"

Delia answered with a smile. "Here."

"Smiling and prepared, as usual, I see." Miss Benson liked her, Delia could tell. Delia knew most of her teachers liked her because she was always pleasant and cooperative, willing to run errands or pass out materials. "Are you jumping on the Double Dutch team again this year?"

"Oh, yeah—it's the bomb!" Yolanda blurted out before Delia had a chance to answer. "Me and Delia and Charlene Byrd are the best jumpers on the face of the earth! You oughta come see us jump tomorrow! It's just the city qualifying competition, but I'll still be dynamite! Or you can come to the state finals in a few weeks if you feel like driving to Columbus."

Delia turned around and grinned at Yolanda, who always enjoyed being the center of attention. She also noticed that the Tolliver brothers had glanced at each other as Yolanda spoke. Delia's smile faded into a frown.

Miss Benson replied, "I'm very proud of all of you, but I can't come tomorrow. However, I promise I will come to see you jump one of these days."

"Okay, then plan to come to the national finals—well, we call it the World Championships because kids from places like Taiwan and Canada and Germany come here to compete. They're gonna be held here in Cincinnati in a couple of months. And I WILL be the star!" she boasted with a grin. "I'll let you know the dates and stuff."

Miss Benson promised again to try to make it. The rest of the class started to talk about the Double Dutch team, the baseball team, the choir—the conversation expanding as each person added something about their own particular after-school activity.

"Let's settle down now," Miss Benson said mildly. She continued through the rest of the names on the list, even though she could see at a glance who was absent. It was her way of making the class feel comfortable. Delia liked the fact that Miss Benson took the time to talk to the kids, even if it was just stupid small talk before each class.

"Leeza Moxley? Nice hairstyle this morning."

Leeza smiled and stood for everyone to notice her curls and waves. Most of the kids ignored her, but Leeza didn't care. She had been given a chance to show off.

"Miss Yolanda Pepper," Miss Benson said with a little bow, as if Yo Yo were some kind of princess. Yolanda loved it, of course. "What a lovely necklace," Miss Benson began.

"I got it in Mexico when me and my parents went this weekend," Yolanda said immediately. "It's real silver."

"My parents and I," Miss Benson said automatically. Then she asked, "You went to Mexico just for the weekend?" Delia laughed to herself. She couldn't believe that Miss Benson could keep falling for Yolanda's tall tales. Yolanda, who liked to be called Yo Yo, specialized in not telling the truth.

"Hey, Miss Benson, you ought to know you can't believe Yo Yo. She lies like a rug! She ain't never been to Mexico. And she got that necklace at the dollar store!" Randy shouted loudly across the room.

"Now you just telling everybody where you buy your clothes!" Yolanda retorted.

Randy grinned and yelled back, "No, but I saw your mama there. She's so backwards, she was askin' for a price check at the dollar store!"

double dutch

"Don't you be talkin' about my mama, Randy! I was in Mexico and I can prove it," Yolanda insisted. "I'll show you my plane ticket stub!" Yolanda furiously dug in her purse, searching for the paper that would prove her story. "I can't find it, but I'll bring it tomorrow. You can call my mother and ask her!"

"Your mama probably don't even know where Mexico is!" Randy teased. "Your mama is so dumb, she couldn't pass a blood test!" Everyone in the class laughed, except for the Tollivers.

Yo Yo put her hands on her hips and fired a look of challenge at Randy. "I told you don't be talkin' about my mother! Your mama's so backwards she sits on the TV and watches the couch!"

Randy quipped back quickly, "Well, your mama's so clumsy she got tangled up in the cordless phone!"

"Well, I heard your mama took a spoon to the Super Bowl!"

"That's enough from both of you!" Miss Benson said sternly. "I will NOT have this kind of disrespect in my classroom!" She was quickly losing control of the class. Delia watched with mild amusement.

As she sat down, Yolanda muttered loud enough for Randy to hear, "At least I got a mama!" Randy's smile faded. He tried to hide it, but Delia could see the hurt look on his face.

Miss Benson went back to taking attendance. "Tabu Tolliver?" The room was silent. "I see you're here. Good," Miss Benson said.

"Titan Tolliver? Also present," Miss Benson said, almost to herself. She looked a little nervous, Delia thought. "Randy Youngblood? As if I need to ask!"

"Yo!" Randy shouted loudly. "The Youngblood is here! And I'm sorry for all that stuff I said, Miss Benson. Yolanda's mama is cool with me." He was trying to regain a little power, Delia realized. Yolanda had been way out of line. Randy's mother had left her husband and her son a couple of years ago. Randy had not heard from her since, and even though he tried to cover it up with jokes, Delia knew it still was a painful subject for him.

"Sit down, Randy. Nobody could miss you. And your apology should go to Yolanda." Randy glanced at Yolanda, but she had taken a brush from her book bag and was noticeably fixing her hair while ignoring Randy completely.

"That's everyone. Let's get started." Miss Benson began by passing out several typed pages that had come from the school office. "Put the brush away, Yolanda. Your hair looks fine." Without pausing to make sure Yolanda did as she was told, Miss Benson continued: "As you know, class, the state proficiency test is coming up soon. It's extremely important for you as eighth graders because it will determine if you go on to ninth grade. We've been practicing and preparing all year for this, and I know you're ready—I'm confident you'll all do fine. Take these information forms home to your parents and bring them back signed on Monday. The test is next month. Are there any questions? Yes, Randy?"

"What if I fail?"

"You're not going to fail. You're the biggest, smartest thing in here!" Miss Benson said, laughing.

"I think so too. And the best-looking, too! I just wanted to hear you say it!"

"Sit down, Randy."

Delia loved the way Randy always made class fun. He

joked around and teased all the teachers. But he always made good grades—straight A's.

"Miss Benson?"

"Yes, Yolanda?" Miss Benson sighed. Delia could tell this was not what the teacher had planned for today's class. But Delia didn't care; anything that stalled real academic work was fine with her.

"I can't take the test," Yolanda began as she stuffed the brush into her book bag and took out a small mirror to check the results.

"Why not?"

"I read an article that said excessive testing causes blood clots in the brain. I can't afford to risk my health for a stupid test. I am a champion Double Dutch jumper, you know."

"I'll pay for your hospitalization," Miss Benson zapped back at her.

She's learning, Delia thought. Delia asked no questions. She looked at the forms, found the line marked with an X for the parental signature, and expertly signed her mother's name on the information sheet. She had memorized both of her parents' signatures long ago. Then she stuffed the forms into her book bag.

The rest of the class asked lots of questions, mostly to delay the start of the lesson. Miss Benson tried to answer every one, seemingly unaware of their delaying tactics. Finally she said, "Okay, that's enough on that. Class, get out your notebooks. Let's get started."

Tabu and Titan glared at her in a stony silence from the back of the room. They did not move, and Miss Benson said nothing to them. She looked as if she was trying to pretend that they weren't there. But they never took their eyes off the teacher. It seemed to Delia that they weren't watching Miss Benson to learn but were checking her out for something more sinister. She seemed to be uncomfortable with their hard, unflinching stares, and she made a big deal of passing out books and checking book cards. Delia noticed that she looked everywhere except at the twins in the back of the room. But they never stopped watching her.

Delia turned her attention from Tabu and Titan to the new book that the teacher was introducing. The old familiar feeling of dread filled her stomach as Miss Benson began the lesson. Delia took out her notebook and pretended to take notes, but what she wrote was in handwriting so tiny that no one could see what she was writing. But even with a magnifying glass no one could have read what Delia had written. It was all tiny scribble.

They were starting a book called *Lord of the Flies*—something about kids in a jungle, she figured from the picture on the front. *I've got to see if there's a videotape of this,* Delia thought. She flipped through the pages and sighed as line after incomprehensible line of gray text stared back at her. She recognized many of the words—the shorter ones, and the words that were easy to identify or memorize. But sometimes even those danced around the page like unruly children. Sometimes an easy word like "boy" looked like "yob." And sometimes it looked like the whole page was written in Martian. She sighed, frowned, and listened carefully to every word Miss Benson was saying. She had an excellent memory and could sometimes tell the teacher word for word what had been said in class the day before. But Delia couldn't read.

two

RANDY WAS THINKING OF DELIA AS HE LET HIMSELF INTO the small apartment he shared with his father. Delia seemed to have it all together, he thought—she was smart, pretty, and never made a fool of herself in class like he did sometimes.

A skinny gray cat stretched and jumped off the kitchen table, where she knew she shouldn't have been sleeping. Randy ignored the cat, tossed his book bag on the floor, took off his shoes and socks, and walked around barefoot on the cool floor. He loved to walk barefoot, and since there was no one there except the cat to complain about his stinky feet, he allowed himself to do as he pleased.

Randy had just turned fourteen, and he already stood over six feet tall. He carried his two hundred pounds with ease, but he stayed hungry. Large meals seemed to last only a few minutes before he was starving again. School lunches were a joke to Randy's huge appetite. His father had told him once, "Boy, you're just like that gas-guzzling truck I got—can't keep either one of you filled up!"

Randy fixed himself five bologna sandwiches, using the last of the bread, even the ends, and started to pour a glass of milk. He looked at the glass, shook his head, then put it back in the cupboard and drank directly from the carton.

He noticed that the carton was nearly empty. He found two large bags of potato chips and three Twinkies in another cupboard and took his snack to the next room to watch TV. He stretched out on the sofa, idly flicking the remote control while he gobbled his food. He paused at one of the afternoon talk shows. The announcer was saying, "We now return to 'Teens Who Terrify'!" Randy had seen many talk shows like this. The host would interview parents who couldn't handle their impossible teenagers, who were unbelievably rude or vicious or dangerous. Today a twelve-year-old dressed like a twenty-five-year-old stripper was cursing at her mother, every other word bleeped out by the TV station. The mother, who did not even try to correct the behavior, simply sat there and cried. "Kid needs her butt kicked," Randy said to the cat. Another young girl, dressed in an outfit her mother said she wore to school—a skimpy tank top and a skirt that was short enough to be called underwear—pranced around the stage as if she was proud of what she was wearing. Her mother wept also. "This couldn't be real—they've gotta be actors. Where do they get this stuff?" Randy complained to the cat, who had her eyes on what was left of Randy's bologna sandwiches.

He watched as more parents reported how their children beat them or stole from them or stayed out all weekend getting drunk. "Unbelievable," Randy muttered. "This is so fake!" The cat had decided to join him on the sofa.

"Our next guests," the host announced with pumped-up excitement, using that phony, oily voice that only TV announcers use, "are twins who terrify their whole neighborhood!" Randy reached for the remote, figuring that even reruns of *Barney* were better than this, but suddenly the camera was focused on the unsmiling faces of Tabu and Titan Tolliver.

Randy jumped up, knocked over the carton of milk onto the floor, dropped the rest of his last sandwich, and ran to the telephone. The cat pounced on the sandwich and the spilled milk while Randy frantically dialed Yolanda's number.

"Yolanda!" Randy said breathlessly. "Turn on Channel Twelve! Quick!"

"I already have it on. I was on three-way with Charlene and Delia, and we're all looking at it! I'll call you back! I'm taping it!"

Randy turned the volume up loud and sat back on the couch, stunned. These weren't actors—these were real people. From his school. From his third-bell English class. "Unbelievable!" he muttered again, but this time it was for a completely different reason.

The commercial ended, and Mrs. Tolliver, the twins' mother, a thin, tired-looking woman, showed pictures of them as three-year-olds—identically chubby little boys staring at the camera with faint smiles. The TV camera then focused on Tabu and Titan as teenagers, dressed in their usual black, looking defiant and uncaring. Randy listened in amazed silence.

HOST: So tell me, Mrs. Tolliver, how long have you been having problems with these two young men of yours?

MRS. TOLLIVER: Well, Preston, I think it started when they were born. I didn't even know I was carrying twins.

They were preemies—really tiny and sickly at birth. I went into labor early, and they were born at home. By the time I was able to get to the hospital, both babies needed oxygen. Maybe they missed something important those first few minutes of life. Maybe it's my fault.

HOST: Let's not place any blame here, Mrs. Tolliver. What happened next?

MRS. TOLLIVER: I took them home, but it was a struggle just to find enough food for them. My husband had been laid off, and we couldn't pay the rent. We moved around a lot. It was awful.

HOST: How did they act as infants? How did they react to others when they were kids?

MRS. TOLLIVER: They were scrawny little things, but they were happy babies, I guess. Seemed like they just focused on each other and left me out, though. They cried when they were hungry, and sometimes that was pretty often. I feel so bad. I loved my babies—I didn't want to be a bad mother, but I never felt I was giving them what they needed. When they got old enough, and I found me a job, I sent them to day care. I figured maybe they needed socialization. They didn't seem to like anything or anybody but each other.

HOST: Did day care help?

MRS. TOLLIVER: Not really. The teachers complained

that they refused to play with the other children—only with each other. Plus, sometimes they would hit other children, and the teachers said they broke toys on purpose. I had to take them out. I don't think it was their fault, though.

HOST: What do you mean—not their fault?

MRS. TOLLIVER: They couldn't cope with their father's death. How do you explain to three-year-olds that their daddy is dead?

HOST: Did you ever seek professional help for them?

MRS. TOLLIVER: I didn't have money for that.

HOST: How did their father die?

MRS. TOLLIVER: In a storm. I don't want to talk about it. Look, I work hard and I've tried to do my best for my boys. But I guess I'm failing.

HOST: Don't cry, now. We're going to see if we can get you some help. What happened when the boys got to kindergarten?

MRS. TOLLIVER: I moved from Minnesota to California when they were five. But it was all the same stuff. Even worse. I moved around quite a bit, trying to find work for me and a place they could be happy at, a place where they could just be kids. But it just got worse. I've moved to seven states in seven years. Maybe that's the problem. We just moved to Ohio, and so far there's been no real incidents, at least that I know of.

TABU: That's 'cause you don't know everything.

TITAN: Some stuff you don't need to know.

HOST: Let's talk to these young men. Your names are rather unusual. I don't think I've ever met anyone with names that are so . . . strong.

TITAN: Our daddy named us.

TABU: He wanted us to be tough.

MRS. TOLLIVER: Maybe things would have turned out differently if their father had lived.

HOST: Are you aware of the pain you've caused your mother?

TABU AND TITAN: So what?

HOST: So she's your mother, and she obviously loves you very much, and your behavior hurts her—deeply.

TABU AND TITAN: Oh, well.

HOST: I notice you answered together. Do you often do that?

TABU AND TITAN: Yeah.

HOST: You say there are things your mother doesn't know about. Things like what?

TABU: We're always getting blamed for stuff, whether we did it or not.

TITAN: So we just decided to make it come true. Just wait and see.

HOST: I don't understand. Can you help our TV audience understand what you mean? What you say is very disturbing and rather frightening.

TABU: Isn't that why you've got us on this show?

HOST: No, we're here to try and help you, and your mother.

TITAN: Don't need no help. Just watch out. Leave us alone and nobody gets hurt.

HOST: What do you mean?

TABU: Don't mean nothin'. Stuff happens.

HOST: Are you just saying these things because you're on TV? Or are they real threats? These days, statements like yours have to be taken very seriously.

TABU: We ain't threatened nobody. We're on TV because our mother told us she'd pay us if we showed up.

TITAN: And 'cause can't nobody beat us, so who cares?

HOST: Is this true, Mrs. Tolliver? Did you bribe them to come on the show?

MRS. TOLLIVER: I, I, didn't know what else to do. I need help. The producers told me I could maybe get some psychological help for my boys if I got them to come on the show. I'd do anything to save my boys.

TABU: Save us?

TITAN: From what?

HOST: From yourselves. From jail. From death.

TITAN: Everybody gotta die.

TABU: Even you.

HOST: I think it's time to break for a commercial. We'll be back after these messages.

Randy sat stunned in front of the TV. These guys needed to be locked up or something.

The phone rang, making him jump. It was Delia. "Did you see that? What are we going to do?"

"There's nothing we *can* do. There's no law against talking bad or being mean."

"You mean we just have to wait until they do something terrible? Can't the school do something?"

"Probably not. We just gotta be careful. Especially you girls. Don't be walking alone after school."

"You don't have to warn me! Did they say somebody's gonna die?"

"Not exactly. They never really said what they would do, or even might do. It sounded like it was part of an act."

"It worked. I'm scared."

Randy took a deep breath. "I'll take care of you, Delia."

"Really?"

"For real. I got your back."

"Thanks, Randy," Delia said quickly. "You make me feel real good. Hey, I gotta go. My other line is beeping. I know it's Charlene or Yo Yo."

"Later."

Randy got a dish towel and wiped up what the cat had missed from the floor. He wondered how big a threat the Tolliver twins could be. And he thought about Delia and how much he liked her. He chuckled to himself. He never would have had the nerve to talk to Delia like that if the Tollivers hadn't freaked everybody out. He picked up the cat, who was now asleep on the kitchen table. But there was some stuff he couldn't tell Delia or anybody else—stuff like he didn't know where his dad was. He was getting really worried. He hadn't seen his father in six weeks. He was running out of money and food. He was all alone. Except for the cat.

three

THE NEXT MORNING AT SCHOOL, EVERYONE WAS BUZZING about the Tollivers being on television. The twins were absent from school, which fed the fears and rumors even more.

"I heard they were planning to blow up the school!" asserted Yolanda, as if she had been told directly by one of the twins.

"You did not!" Delia retorted. "Don't be starting no mess, Yo Yo."

"Well, they could have," Yolanda replied. "Who knows what they said after the show went off the air."

"We just better watch our backs!" Jesse said. "Threatening folks on national TV!"

Yolanda, pleased that Jesse, her latest love interest, was close enough in the hall to join the conversation, laughed, looked directly at him, and said, "You are so right."

"Did they really threaten anybody?" Delia asked thoughtfully. No one answered her.

"I DID hear that the teachers held an emergency meeting this morning," Yolanda told the collected students in the hall. "I bet we get metal detectors and police in the halls!"

"I bet they're scared," Charlene said. "I sure am. I have two classes with the Tollivers."

"Me too," said Delia. She glanced at Randy, who smiled at her. It made her feel safe.

"Have they actually DONE anything?" Randy asked. "Does anybody have any proof of anything bad they have done? Anybody?"

Everyone was silent. But the fear remained nevertheless. The rest of the school day tiptoed by while everyone waited nervously for the return of the Tollivers.

Delia watched Yolanda breeze through her first few classes. Delia, however, felt every class was a struggle and was beginning to feel overwhelmed with the amount of work the teachers were requiring, and the amount of work it took to figure how to get around it all.

She and Yolanda walked down the back steps of the school toward an unoccupied bench. Lunch followed Miss Benson's English class, and when the weather was nice they usually ate together outside rather than in the hot and crowded lunchroom.

Yolanda carefully unwrapped her egg salad sandwich and announced, "I shouldn't be eating this. I'm allergic to eggs, you know."

Delia said nothing.

"The last time I ate eggs I broke out in spots and my whole body swelled up like a balloon. My doctor told me the only cure was to eat gallons of chocolate to counteract the disease, so I will be forced to eat five candy bars after lunch!"

Delia usually enjoyed Yolanda's stories because they were silly and they kept her laughing, but today she didn't even smile.

Yo Yo never told the truth. Never had. Delia had

learned to live with it—even looked forward to the latest tall tale that Yo Yo would come up with. They had known each other since first grade, when Yolanda, a six-year-old with extremely long braids, sat down next to Delia and said, "My name is Yo-lan, and I'm from Mars."

"Well, I'm Delia, and I'm from Cincinnati."

"Boring," replied Yolanda. "Mars has bright orange-striped skies. And thirteen moons."

"Weird," mumbled Delia. But they became friends because Yolanda turned ordinary days into adventure stories. Through the years she had told Delia of her father's village in Africa, her summers spent in homeless shelters, and her mother's job as an airline pilot. None of it was true.

At first Delia was annoyed at Yolanda's constant exaggerations and tall tales, but after many visits to Yolanda's house, Delia figured that Yolanda lied because the truth about her life just wasn't very pretty. Yo Yo's father was loud and demanding—a former army man—and her mother always seemed to have either a cigarette or a drink in her hand when she came to the door.

"Why you look so bummed out, girl?" Yolanda asked finally. "Every time Miss Benson starts talking about the state proficiency test, you act like she's announcing that all the Shoe Carnival stores are going out of business!"

"It's nothing. I just hate tests," Delia replied, nibbling on a carrot stick.

"I remember in elementary school, seems like you were always absent on days we had big tests."

"Maybe."

"This stupid test is really no big deal. We took it last

year for practice, remember? It was a piece of cake. I passed all five sections—first try, didn't you?"

"No."

"I thought you told me you passed it too."

"I probably did tell you that. But I didn't. I failed it. All of it." She looked at Yolanda. "All except the math part," Delia added quietly.

"Well, it's not important. It was just a practice test. I'm sure you'll do okay on the real thing."

"I don't want to talk about it."

"Okay. It's cool. Hey! I almost forgot! I got something I want to show you. Look what Jesse got me for my birthday!" Yolanda dug in her book bag and pulled out a tiny box of candy and a pink, flower-decorated greeting card.

"Dude musta robbed a bank—spent all of three dollars for the card and the candy!" Delia laughed as she sipped her juice.

"It's the thought that counts!" Yolanda insisted. "Read the card! It must have taken him a long time to find a card that said just what I wanted to hear!"

"You sure you didn't buy it yourself? Seems like I remember last Valentine's Day, you bought yourself ten Valentines and swore you had ten boyfriends!"

"That was last year when I was a child of thirteen and before I met my true love, Jesse."

"Your true love? You don't know anything about him!"

"I'll find out if I decide I like him well enough to ask. 'Never waste too much time on eighth-grade boys' is my motto. But Jesse's got potential. He's got a bit of class—enough to pick out such a cool gift."

"He coulda picked up the first card with hearts and flowers he saw and you woulda loved it! Your brain is noodle soup when it comes to boys."

"Read it. Read it. I want to hear it out loud!" Yolanda jumped up from the bench and pretended she was holding a microphone. "Ladies and gentlemen! Words of love from Jesse Johnson to the lovely Yolanda Pepper!"

Delia frowned. "I don't feel like it. Read your own stupid card." She jerked away and started to stuff her uneaten sandwich back into the brown paper bag.

Yo Yo looked sharply at Delia, like she was determined to say something. She took a deep breath and asked, "Why, Delia?"

"I just don't want to. I left my glasses at home. Leave me alone!" The softness of the sunny day was destroyed. Delia shifted uncomfortably. They still had fifteen minutes before the bell rang for the next class. "I gotta go to the bathroom. I'll see you after school." She started to get up from the bench.

"Delia?" Yolanda looked directly at her friend.

"What?" Delia looked at the sky.

"We've been best friends since first grade, right?"

"Yeah, I guess."

"You were there for me in third grade when my baby sister died."

"Yeah, that was rough."

"And I stood by you through all that mess when your mom and dad got divorced when we were in fourth grade."

"Yeah. So?"

"So it's okay if you admit to me, and only me, your very best friend, your secret."

"What secret?"

"The only thing we have never talked about." Yolanda sighed and continued. "I know you can't read, Delia. I've known for a long time."

Silence. Delia sat back down on the bench, stunned. Yolanda sat next to her. Cars whizzed by in the street beyond the teachers' parking lot. Echoes of shouts from the lunchroom drifted toward them. A bird chirped nervously in a tree. An airplane flew overhead. But Delia was silent. She thought of denying it, but she was so tired of hiding, tired of pretending. She covered her eyes, and let her shoulders drop, and finally she began to cry.

This time Yolanda was silent. She waited.

"Then why'd you stick that card in my face?" Delia asked finally, wiping her nose on her sleeve.

"Fakin' it. Just like you been doin'."

"You won't tell?" Delia asked after a moment.

"Who am I gonna tell? And who would believe me anyway? Everybody knows how much I lie."

"You got that right."

"I don't know how you managed to get this far without being able to read and without anybody figuring it out."

"I fooled *you*, didn't I?"

"For a while. I sat right next to you through most of elementary school. I thought you were reading, at first."

"Mostly I was copying off your paper."

"Get outta here!" Yolanda pretended she was shocked. "Seriously, I guess I knew, even before I really figured it all out, but how'd you fool all the teachers?"

Delia sighed. "It was easy in elementary school. That school was a mess. Teacher parade. Remember? Miss Pringle in fourth grade got pregnant and left. Then Mr. Balboa took her place, and all he did was read the newspaper while we played cards and checkers."

Yolanda nodded. "In fifth grade we had that long-term sub until Thanksgiving—the one who kept falling asleep in class—Mr. Biski."

"Yeah, old Biscuit Head Biski!" Delia laughed. "Then the lady they finally hired quit by January—I don't even remember her name—said her nerves couldn't take thirty-five fifth graders. And the new lady was so confused, she never learned our names. If we did purple ditto sheets and shut up, we passed."

Yolanda grinned. "Yeah, that was the life!"

Delia sighed again. "In sixth grade Mrs. Davenport decided to retire early, so we got Mr. Franklin, who got fired for smacking Willie Williams in the face."

"I don't blame him. Willie Williams was a pig," Yolanda asserted. "But then we had another long-term sub . . ."

". . . Who never figured out I had a problem," Delia said, finishing Yo Yo's thought. "I guess I was just lucky in elementary school."

"Or maybe really unlucky. Somebody could have helped you back then."

"I didn't need any help. I figured out how to beat the system."

"Yeah, but now the system is about to beat your butt!" Yolanda repacked her book bag and brushed her hair. She clearly enjoyed showing off the fact that she had hair that was long enough to bounce and swing. "You know, it's amazing nobody noticed you always made D's and F's in stuff that required reading."

"I was happy when I got a C on a test," Delia admitted. "But I always did my homework."

"Mostly you did MY homework!" Yolanda laughed and tossed the brush back into her bag.

"Well, what are friends for?" Delia smiled sadly. "And I faked it a lot."

"Yeah, I know. 'Cause you seem smart, and you can memorize better than anyone I know."

"Yolanda, I AM smart. I am NOT dumb!" Delia's anger and frustration returned. "I just can't figure out what the words say sometimes!"

"So that's why you always had to go to the bathroom when we had to read out loud."

"Or I'd get sick."

"With a coughing spell."

"Or I'd fake the hiccups."

"Or you'd cry."

"Or I'd speak so softly that the teacher couldn't hear me."

"Or you'd say you forgot your glasses."

"I never needed glasses."

"You didn't?" This time, Yolanda sounded genuinely shocked.

"My parents were worried when the second-grade teacher told them I was having trouble seeing the board. That was the last really good teacher we had. I could SEE just fine. I just couldn't read it. So when they gave me the eye test, I pretended I couldn't see very well, and I got glasses. Actually, they make everything worse!" Delia laughed as she sniffled.

"Delia," Yolanda said gently as she placed her hand on her friend's shoulder, "I could, uh, maybe help you after

27

school or something. We could, like, you know, get some, like, uh—"

"Books with bunnies and butterflies? Thanks, but no way. It's too late." Delia put her head in her hands.

"How'd you fool your parents?" Yolanda asked finally.

Delia's shoulders slumped. She said nothing to Yolanda for several minutes, thinking back to third grade, when her parents had fought every night. Her father, always coming home late from work, and her mother, fretful and distracted, waiting by the door. Nights were filled with arguments and accusations—yelling, crying, cursing. It was awful. They had tried to keep it in their bedroom, but Delia could hear everything. Delia found out later that her father had been seeing another woman and wanted a divorce.

She could tell her mother was too unhappy to really notice her daughter. Sure, she made sure that Delia had clean clothes and a good dinner and lunch money and that sort of stuff, but she just didn't have the energy to check homework or become involved in school activities. And when Delia was in fourth grade, her father had moved out and her mother was dealing with lawyers and trying to find a second job. Delia remembered that her mother had cried a lot. And she remembered trying to be brave and not wanting to bother her. She figured her mother had enough problems anyway.

"Delia? You okay?" Yolanda asked gently.

"Yeah." Delia sighed. "I guess I'm just dead meat."

"Speaking of dead meat, here comes Randy," Yolanda said, smiling at him. Randy grinned as he headed toward the two girls. He was carrying three cookies wrapped in plastic.

"Now why you want to dis me like that? And I come bringin' you fresh-baked cafeteria cookies!"

"The only thing fresh-baked from that cafeteria is the dirt!" Yolanda quipped. "And I'm the one who ought to be bringing you gifts. I didn't mean to hurt your feelings in class yesterday."

"Just to show you I forgive you, I'm gonna eat all these cookies myself!" Randy squeezed his large body between the two girls, unwrapped the cookies, and stuffed all three into his mouth at the same time. They laughed as he licked his fingers and the plastic wrap, too.

"You're gross, Randy," Delia said, giggling, glad for the distraction.

"I saw this world record TV show where a man ate a hundred cookies at one time," Yolanda began. "He choked and died right there on live TV."

"You're hopeless, Yolanda," Randy said, laughing. "Everything you say is a lie!"

"At least I'm predictable!" Yolanda retorted. "Let's go to class." The bell rang, and the three of them headed back to the building. "You going to Double Dutch practice tonight, Delia?"

"No way I'm gonna miss it. I want to practice those new moves for the freestyle routine. It's our last chance to get ready for the qualifying championships. City finals are Saturday, you know."

"Bet we've got a good chance to go all the way this year."

"I'll be there too," Randy added. "Gotta watch you ladies do your thing!"

"You're just lucky we let you hang around such fine young things!" Yolanda teased as she tossed her ponytail in his face. Randy laughed and bounded down the hall to his class.

Delia was quiet as she watched him disappear down the hall. She had trouble acting silly around Randy. He made her feel sweaty and self-conscious. But it wasn't Randy who was making her armpits feel clammy today. It was the test. It was rumbling down the road like a runaway truck, and she was standing, helpless, directly in its path.

four

DELIA WAS GLAD SHE HAD DOUBLE DUTCH ON SATUR-day. It took her mind off the threats of tests and twins, and worries about reading and homework. When they were younger, all of the girls had jumped rope for fun on the city sidewalks during summer vacations—doubles, singles, twirls, fancy jumps, and trick moves—each showing off to impress one another, as well as the boys who had always gathered to watch from a distance when they took a break from playing basketball. But *this* was official Double Dutch, sponsored by the American Double Dutch League. It had official rules, standards, and regulations, with teams for kids as young as third grade, and even a senior division for adults who wanted to jump.

Delia and Yolanda hurried into the gym at the recreation center where Double Dutch practices and events were held. They had practice at least three times a week after school or in the evening, but this Saturday morning event was the first qualifying tournament of the year—the one that led to the state and national championships. Teams from all over Cincinnati were meeting today to decide which of the participants would compete at the next level.

Charlene had just arrived, and the three friends, dressed in shorts, tennis shoes, and matching navy blue Double

Dutch T-shirts, tossed their gym bags in a corner, pulled out their practice ropes, and began their warm-up stretches and practice jumps. Around the noisy gym, dozens of other jumpers from ages eight to eighteen were doing the same.

"Let's practice compulsories," Delia suggested, "before Randy and Bomani get here." Bomani was their coach, and Randy was equipment manager. Randy really seemed to enjoy his job, and Delia was sure it had something to do with hanging around a gym full of girls.

She got into position, signaled to Yo Yo and Charlene, and took a deep breath. For Delia, jumping was more than exercise—it was magic as she stepped and jumped gracefully in between the twirling ropes. Yolanda and Charlene turned, going through the standard moves for the compulsory part of their routine, which included two clockwise right turns on the right foot, two counterclockwise left turns on the left foot, four crisscross jumps, and ten high step jumps with their knees lifted up to waist level, sung to a chant.

"One-TWO
One-TWO/Three-FOUR!/Five-SIX/Seven-
EIGHT
One-TWO

"One-TWO
One-TWO/Three-FOUR/Five-SIX/Seven-
EIGHT
One-TWO
"Right over left / Left over right / One-TWO

"Now HIGH!
TWO!
THREE!
FOUR!
FIVE!
SIX!
SEVEN!
EIGHT!
NINE!
TEN!
One-TWO–Exit!"

Delia jumped out of the ropes with skill, barely out of breath. She could do this with her eyes closed now.

Two girls from a recreation center across town sauntered over to them. The first girl, who was short, sturdy, and looked like she could punch out a grizzly bear, said nothing at first, but her friend, who was tall and thin, giggled a little as they approached them.

"You been jumping long?" the giggling girl asked Delia.

"I've been jumping on the Queen Bees Double Dutch team since fifth grade," Delia replied, yawning as if she were bored. "What about you?"

"I been jumping since I could walk. My mama runs our team. My name is Shana, and this here is Jackie. What's yours?"

"I'm Yolanda, she's Charlene, and this is Delia," Yo Yo replied. "I've been jumping since I was eight, and I bet Delia can outjump you."

Delia glanced at Yolanda as if to say, "Why you wanna

33

do me like that?" but she said nothing and continued to stretch. Charlene grinned. She knew what was coming.

After Yolanda started jumping with the team when she was eight, she had always asked Delia to come with her to practice at the YMCA gym, but Delia never really believed that Yolanda was on a team, because Yo Yo talked about competitions in Madagascar and Greenland. When Delia finally realized that the team was real and the competitions were held in ordinary places like Columbus, Ohio, she went to one practice and was hooked. She loved the feel of the ropes in her hands and the sensation of electricity when she jumped. And she loved a challenge. Shana and Jackie had shown up just in time.

"Challenge you to a speed jump?" Delia asked casually.

"Bet," Shana and Jackie answered together. Shana giggled nervously while Jackie took a deep breath and got ready to enter the ropes.

Delia and Yolanda turned while Jackie jumped. Charlene and Shana pretended to ignore each other. The turners started off slowly, turning in time with Jackie's feet, and as her speed increased, so did the whirling of the ropes over her head, so that soon nothing could be heard but the tapping of her shoes and the whirling of the ropes as they made a breeze in the corner of the gym.

Jackie finally missed, jumping out and laughing, taking the ropes from Delia so she could take a turn. Nobody had really counted the number of jumps, or even timed them—it was the challenge of the speed and the ropes that they jumped for. It was all in fun, but deadly serious at the same time.

Delia missed after just a few jumps, and so did Charlene, but when it was Yolanda's turn, she was jumping so fast and so well that even Shana and Jackie were cheering for her.

When she finally jumped out of the ropes, she said, laughing, "Don't be hatin', girlfriends. You know I'm bad!" The five girls laughed and chatted as if they were old friends. They all got some water, then Shana and Jackie wandered back to the other side of the gym. Delia knew the day would be fun as well as challenging.

Delia hopped back into the ropes, jumping easily while Charlene and Yolanda turned, when Yolanda laughed and started reciting a chant that they had all jumped to as kids.

"Down in the valley where the green grass grows,
There sat Dee Dee as sweet as a rose,
She sang, she sang, she sang so sweet,
Along came Randy and kissed her on the cheek!
How many kisses did she receive?
Was it one, two—"

"Stop, girl! I'm not jumpin' if you want to be playin' like that. We don't have time for kids' games. The championship is coming up. Besides, why you want to put Randy's name in the chant?" Delia jumped out of the ropes, tossed a towel on her head, and strode over to the cooler to get some more water. Her hair, cut short like a cap on her head, felt damp and sticky from the hair spray she used to keep it from jumping up and down when she did. She laughed as Yolanda and Charlene kept turning and singing. "You know the rules. You're s'posed to put the ropes down when I jump out."

They ignored her. Yolanda, who stood with her knees slightly bent and her legs slightly bowed, never took her eyes from the ropes that whipped and popped on the shiny gym floor. "One, two, three, four, five, six, seven, eight. . . . Girlfriend, you gonna catch something, kissin' on that boy like that. He told me he loved you, you know. You heard him, didn't you, Charlene? He was standing right over there by the gym door. Last night. About eight o'clock. Remember?" Yolanda waited for Charlene to back up her story.

Charlene dropped her end of the ropes, scratched her head, and said, "Yo Yo, you trippin', girl. He never said no such thing. Randy wasn't even here last night. For that matter, neither were you! We didn't have practice yesterday! Remember?"

Yolanda slapped herself on the side of her head and said, as if she had just remembered, "Oh that flu shot. The doctors told me that it would cause memory loss and hallucinations. I think I'm feeling faint, too. Anybody got some cough drops? The doctor told me to eat plenty of cough drops. It fools the flu, you know. Makes your body think that you're really sick, when all you're doing is fakin' it by chewing on cough drops. Brilliant, huh? Anyway, I know Randy wants him some Delia. I can feel it when he walks by her." Yo Yo tossed her hair so that it swung round from her back to the front and back again. She liked it long and refused to tie it up for practice or meets, even after the time her hair got caught in the ropes during a jump. She had told the coach that cutting her hair or tying it up was against her religion. The coach hadn't believed her, but hadn't brought the matter up again.

Delia just shook her head and ignored Yolanda as she drank her water. "I'm not thinkin' about Randy," Delia finally said as she walked back over the ropes. "He makes me itch. Just turn the ropes, girl. Let's see if we can get the rhythm. Then we'll switch and each take a turn jumping."

"I bet he wants to scratch that itch," Yo Yo mumbled, but she picked up her end of the ropes and started to turn once more. Charlene laughed, but Delia ignored both of them as she concentrated on keeping up with the whipping of the ropes on the gym floor. She tried to keep her mind blank: ready, open only to feeling the rhythm of the ropes. She didn't think of Randy, who was large and noisy and made her miss a step when she knew he was watching her jump. She didn't think of Yo Yo, who was a dependable, but complicated, friend. And she didn't think about her problems about school. Not today. Her feet danced, and her body leaped with delight as she spun to the rhythm of the ropes. She did not miss for the entire drill, until the back door of the gym flew open and Randy came in with the breeze.

five

RANDY FILLED A ROOM WHEN HE WALKED INTO IT, EVEN A room as large as a gym. At least that's how Delia felt when she saw him come in the back door. He looked like he had everything under control, she thought, with his baseball hat carefully placed so the brim touched the back of his neck, his shoes untied, and his sweatpants pulled down low on his butt, one pant leg down, one pant leg pushed up to his knee. He could have been wearing a sign that read, I REALLY DON'T CARE, she thought.

Delia didn't know too much about Randy except that he lived with his dad, who was a long-distance truck driver. Even though he was often out of town, when Randy's dad had come to a couple of the team's Double Dutch events, Randy had beamed like a lightning bug. She'd heard rumors that Randy's mom had run off with the mailman or something like that, but Delia tried not to pay attention to that kind of talk.

She jumped out of the ropes and knelt to tie her shoelace. She tried to pretend not to notice him. He even smelled good. The faint smell of something woodsy drifted through the air that, just moments before, had smelled merely of old gym and new sweat. Delia knew that for her to be able to smell it clear across the gym, he had to be wearing way too much cologne, but she smiled anyway.

He smiled at Delia as he got out the official ropes and spread them out in pairs on the floor. She smiled back, but suddenly felt self-conscious. She was sweaty from that jump, and her hair, in spite of the hair spray, was a mess.

More of the other jumpers had started to arrive and were stretching their legs, getting ready for the next couple of hours of practice and competition. Randy took attendance, collected money from the fourth- and fifth-grade girls who had sold candy as a fund-raiser, and checked the buzzing timers for their timed jumps. Charlene and Yo Yo followed him around, chattering and giggling about the ropes and school yesterday and why Bomani, their coach, was always late.

"He's late 'cause he knows he's got me to get things set up. All he needs to do is yell at you and get you through this competition. I don't care to do that. I'm the setup man. Then I got the best job in the world. I get to sit back and watch a bunch of girls jump for two hours. Sweet."

Delia watched it all from the corner of the gym, wishing she could be like Yo Yo and Charlene and be silly around Randy.

Bomani arrived, late as usual. Everything about him was huge. His hands could almost encircle a basketball. His broad shoulders supported bulging muscles—from years of work at a lumber company. Delia thought he looked like something out of one of those bodybuilding magazines. He made Randy look like a baby chicken. In spite of his bulk, however, Bomani could jump as swiftly and deftly as any fourth grader. He didn't do it often, but everyone at least once had seen him outjump a tired or lazy twelve-year-old and shame her into jumping faster and cleaner.

Bomani strode into the center of the gym, blew his whistle, and said, "Let's get started! Today we'll pick the jumpers who will compete in the state tournament. Third and fourth graders, get ready for your singles compulsory jumps, speed test, and freestyle jumps. We'll do two grades at a time. Fifth and sixth graders, get ready—you're up next! When we've gone through eighth grade and the high school division, we'll do the whole thing over for the doubles teams. Jumpers, are you ready?"

The tension in the small gym sizzled like dangling electric lines—hot and fiery. Lots of parents sat in the stands, watching and cheering as the various groups and teams filled the floor with the confusion that only an organized sports event can produce.

Everyone found their places, and the younger girls began the familiar jumps and twirls. Delia watched with admiration as the little ones jumped with such intensity. The third graders were cute and surprisingly capable.

"Look at that sweet little baby jumper over there," she said, nudging Yolanda as she pointed to a third grader with big eyes and bulging cheeks. "Look at her face—poor kid is going to explode if she doesn't breathe!"

Yolanda laughed. "Yeah, I remember being that nervous when I was little. And look at the new uniforms that the kids from downtown have this year—they look good!"

Delia nodded and grinned, but said nothing, satisfied to breathe deeply of the tension and the glory of that dirty old gym and the expectant jumpers that filled it.

When the time came for the eighth-grade singles teams to jump, Delia, Charlene, and Yolanda knew they were ready. Delia jumped the compulsory round, never missing a step. For the speed jump, Delia and Yolanda turned while Charlene powered her legs with almost blinding speed, never stopping to glance at the clock, concentrating only on the rhythm of the ropes. She whispered, "YES!" as the judges announced that her score was a dynamite 375. Delia and Yolanda hugged her with glee as she bounded off to the sidelines. "Beat THAT!" she mouthed with a smile across the gym to Jackie, who grinned back.

Delia glanced up into the stands, looking to see if her mother had been able to take the day off to come and watch, when she noticed the shadowy figures of the Tolliver twins sitting at the top of the bleachers. Both wore dark sunglasses. Delia shuddered, as if a cold breeze had blown against her sweaty body, and she looked away. She refused to let anyone interrupt her focus today.

The singles freestyle routine was the most challenging and the one that Delia liked the best. It was always the very last event for the singles competitions. She and Yolanda and Charlene had practiced their routine for hours to make it smooth as ice, adding leaps and twists and special dance movements. They were ready.

Delia and Charlene held the ropes wide and low while Yolanda entered the ropes with a back flip. Sometimes she jumped in doing a leapfrog over Delia's head. It took perfect timing and flexibility. Charlene and Delia moved the ropes low and slowly, never taking their eyes off Yolanda, who switched off in the middle and took the ropes from Delia, who then became the jumper. Delia liked to jump in with a hand flip and bounce. It was like an intricate dance with ropes and legs and jumping bodies. The three girls switched turners in the middle of a jump, did flips and somersaults, and ended it effortlessly in a clean, precise landing to the cheers of the people in the stands. Delia beamed with exultation as the three of them took their seats with the rest of their team. They knew they had done well.

After a short break, Bomani blew his whistle and announced, "Okay, it's time to do it once more, jumpers, but this time it's the doubles competition. We'll do compulsory doubles first, then the doubles time test, and finally, doubles freestyle. Third- and fourth-grade teams, get into place. Judges, get ready." The steps for the doubles compulsory routine were the same as for the singles, but two girls jumped together in unison, and the time was increased from thirty seconds to forty.

Misty, an eighth grader from another school, was the fourth on Delia's doubles team. She was a powerful jumper with strong legs and thick thigh muscles—absolutely essential when they did speed jumps. She was the final jumper in the doubles speed jump, where one jumper entered the ropes and jumped for fifty-five seconds, then the second jumper jumped the remainder of the two-minute test. They could always depend on Misty to catch up on any lost time or misses. She could do three hundred jumps easy, and often did more.

The buzzer sounded, and the doubles speed competition began for eight-year-olds. Two minutes. Two turners. Two jumpers. Double rhythms whipping together on the gym floor. Parents and other volunteers who worked with the teams stood on the gym floor near each team, clickers in hand, counting the number of times that the left foot of each jumper hit the floor in a two-minute period. The little girls tripped on the ropes occasionally, but the look on their faces was that of absolute determination and concentration.

When it was time for the Queen Bees, Delia jumped in easily, then, head down, knees bent, arms raised to her waist, she began the steady rhythm of the jump. Raising her palm to the ceiling was a signal to Charlene and Yolanda to increase the speed of their turns. Fifty-five seconds later, Misty jumped in as Delia jumped out, Misty's feet matching Delia's steps exactly.

Charlene and Yo Yo turned in perfect rhythm with Misty as she peppered the floor with her steps, her arms spinning with the ropes. The girls shouted encouragement as they jumped.

"Go, girl! Pick your feet up! Pick your feet up!"

"Concentrate! Concentrate!"

"You got it! You got it!"

"Thirty seconds! This is it!"

"Faster!" yelled Yolanda. "Faster!" Misty's strong brown legs darted in and out of the ropes as they turned so fast they were spinning shadows, whipping dust as she swiftly and skillfully skipped in and out of the intricate pattern, the rapid sounds of her tennis shoes on the floor of the gym beating in perfect harmony to the drumbeat of the ropes.

The buzzer sounded—like a sheep in pain, as Yolanda had once described it—and Misty jumped nimbly out of the ropes. "How'd we do?" Misty asked the judge who had been timing them.

"Four hundred! Excellent!" the judge said with encouragement.

Delia glanced across the gym at Shana and Jackie. Shana waved and gave a thumbs-up sign that let Delia know that they, too, had done well. Looking into the stands again, Delia finally saw her mother, as well as the twins, who had not moved from their perch at the top.

"Did you see who's here?" Delia whispered to Yolanda. "The Tollivers."

Yolanda glanced at the two and waved. If they saw her, they did not indicate it. "Let 'em look!" she said as she put on fresh lipstick. "I hope they like what they see!"

"You're crazy," Delia muttered. "I gotta keep my focus here."

They finished the eighth-grade doubles freestyle competition. Delia and her team did well, but they made a couple of careless mistakes—not enough to eliminate them, but enough to make them realize they were not invincible.

After a short meeting of the judges, the teams for the state finals were announced. "I can't believe we got picked," Misty exclaimed.

"I knew we would. We're bad!" Delia said with confidence.

"Hey! Shana and Jackie's team is going on to State too," Yolanda said as their team was announced.

"You know, lots of kids get to go to the State finals," Delia commented. "The city competition isn't nearly as fierce as the larger meets. We're gonna have to watch out."

"Well, I'm glad that everybody gets to go to Columbus—even the kids that didn't quite make the cut this year," Yolanda said as she packed her gym bag.

"Yeah, I feel ya," Delia replied. "It's fun being at tournaments and cheering for everybody. It's the team that counts."

The gym emptied quickly after the results were

announced. The Tollivers were nowhere to be seen. Delia felt charged and exultant, but she was tired. She was ready to get out of there and go home. She glanced at Randy, who was collecting all the ropes, putting them in the lockers, and straightening up the gym. She watched while Charlene and Yolanda told him jokes, and decided to ignore them all as she hurried out of the gym and into her mother's car after only brief good-byes.

six

DELIA, YOLANDA, AND CHARLENE SHIVERED IN THE EARLY March breeze on Monday morning, waiting for the first bell to ring.

"I wish winter would hurry up and get out of here. I'm tired of bein' cold," Charlene complained in her thin white slacks and sleeveless blouse.

"Maybe if you wore your winter coat, you wouldn't be freezing your buns off," Yolanda replied as she hugged herself in her heavy coat.

"I'm tired of my winter coat, too!" Charlene laughed. "Cold weather is boring."

"Well, you can't say it's boring around here!" Delia declared. "You think today is the day the Tollivers are going to do something?"

"Well, there's lots of crazy stuff that's been happening at other schools—shootings and killings and stuff. Scares me to death!"

"Don't say 'death'—you're freakin' me out!" Yolanda exclaimed. "I'm scared enough already. You think they'll kick them out of school?" Yolanda had made up no tales about the Tollivers today. The situation was much too tense.

"Probably not. The twins haven't *done* anything, except

talk bad on a dumb TV show. They didn't even threaten anybody," Delia moaned. She saw Randy walk toward them, coming from the bus stop. "Hey, Randy, what's up?"

"Not much. Just the cold. And I'm hungry—I didn't have time to eat breakfast. Any of you lovely ladies got any munchies?" He looked directly at Delia as he spoke.

"So now we're 'lovely ladies,' huh?" Charlene teased.

Delia pulled a Twinkie out of her lunch bag. Randy grabbed it, and with his mouth full, said, "If you got food, you're beautiful!" He smiled at her gratefully. The bell rang, and Charlene darted ahead of them to get into the warmth of the building before the others.

When the Tolliver twins marched in together, everyone cleared a wide path for them in the hall. No one spoke to them or mentioned the TV show.

"My mom told me the teachers met with the school board, the principal, their mother, and community leaders, but since the twins had really done nothing wrong, there was nothing legally that could be done," Delia whispered to Charlene.

"Yeah, I heard that the teachers were told that they had to let them go to class," Charlene whispered back as the two boys passed by.

The twins seemed to know that, and almost smiled as they dominated the halls.

Yolanda, deliberately ignoring the Tollivers, asked Randy, "Your dad on the road again?" She dug in her book bag for a bag of potato chips to give him. "Must be cool to be a long-distance truck driver. You know, before he was an airplane pilot, my dad used to drive a—"

"Don't even start with that, Yolanda," Randy said,

interrupting her. "I got a headache and I don't feel like listening to all that. But thanks for the chips."

Yolanda looked as if she was ready to say something, then she shrugged. "I'll see you both in English. I gotta finish reading the next two chapters of *Lord of the Flies*. It's pretty good." She looked at Delia, as if to offer help if needed, but Delia, with just a slight movement, shook her head to say no. Yolanda disappeared into the crowded hallway.

"You were jumping good on Saturday, Delia," Randy said. "You're dynamite on the speed jump."

"It makes me feel good when I jump—like I got power or something."

"Yeah, I feel ya. Like when I'm playing football and I make a tackle and the little voice from the box comes drifting over the field, 'Tackle! Youngblood!' And I feel like a million dollars. Which I could use right now," he added with a sigh.

"I remember your dad came to every single game you played this fall."

"Yeah, me and my dad are tight," Randy said with a smile. "He fixed his driving schedule so he could be here to see me play. I kept telling him it was just a stupid junior high game, but he said if his boy was in it, it wasn't stupid."

"It must be rough when he's on the road. How long does he stay gone?" Delia asked as they walked to their lockers.

"Oh, usually not more than two or three days. Sometimes, if he gets a special haul, like California, he might be gone for a week, but he tries not to do that. But he always leaves me food and money, and he calls me every night. We got it worked out."

"I admire you," Delia said shyly. "I'd be scared to be at home alone."

"What's to be scared of? Besides, I got my attack cat to protect me," Randy said, laughing. "Home is safe. It's school I'm scared of. Those Tollivers are some scary dudes!"

"You got that right." Delia shivered in spite of the warmth of the overheated halls.

"I meant what I said the other night, Delia." Randy was looking directly at her. "I'll protect you."

Delia had to look away. She was trembling once more, but not from the cold, and not from fear. Randy's voice made her shiver. She smiled at him. "Thanks, Randy. I'll see you in English." He grinned and disappeared up the steps to his next class. Delia glanced at herself in her locker mirror just before she closed the door. She was still smiling.

During her first-bell math class, Delia listened to the buzz of whispers about the Tollivers and their television appearance. The twins arrived late to her math class, with a tardy slip from the office. They said nothing as they tossed the green slip of paper on Mr. Bernaldi's desk. He glanced at them and continued his discussion of polynomials. Another teacher knocked on the door a few minutes later, and the two of them spoke in voices too low for the students to hear, but Delia could see Mr. Bernaldi glancing back at the Tolliver boys. The rest of the students took this brief respite from class to make their own whispered comments.

"I heard they tried to suspend them, but they couldn't."

"I heard the twins are really mad and are gonna get somebody."

Delia said nothing, but she peeked back at Tabu and Titan. They were looking out of the window, seeming to ignore the turmoil, but Delia had a feeling they were enjoying it.

Mr. Bernaldi closed the door and returned to the front of the class. "Let's get back to work, now. Delia, can you tell me the answer to number three?"

Delia glanced at the problem. She thought for the hundredth time how easy math was for her, and wondered why reading was so impossible. "Seventeen," she said with assurance.

"Good job, Delia," Mr. Bernaldi said, smiling. He turned to the twins, a look of challenge and determination on his face. "Tabu, can you tell me the answer to number four?" *Mr. Bernaldi is not about to be intimidated,* Delia thought, turning around in her seat to see what would happen.

"Two forty-nine point five," Tabu replied defiantly, as if answering the challenge. He had barely glanced at his book.

Mr. Bernaldi looked down at his notes to double-check the answer. "You're correct, Tabu," he said quietly. "Good job."

Even though the twins rarely participated in class activities, Delia noticed they made good grades. They were smarter than they let on to be. When teachers passed back papers in grade order from highest to lowest, a practice Delia hated, she noticed that the Tolliver twins usually had papers in the top of the stack and she usually had papers in the bottom. *Maybe if I had a twin,* Delia thought, *I'd get better grades. Two brains have got to be better than one.*

Before Delia's social studies class, the next bell, the students huddled together in small groups, whispering and spreading the little information they knew. Titan and Tabu were not in this class. Then the bell rang, and Mrs. Parks, a tall, powerful African-American woman who wore a colorful African garment to class each day, tossed aside her textbook and said, "Okay, you need to talk, so let's talk. This is what social studies is all about—people and problems. I know you all saw the TV show last week—it always amazes me what you watch when you get home—and I know you are concerned. Without making accusations or false statements, let's discuss what's going on. Melissa? You look worried."

Melissa, a skinny, quiet girl with braces and stringy blond hair, said softly, "I'm afraid of them—the twins."

"Have they ever done anything to make you feel that way?" asked Mrs. Parks.

"No," Melissa admitted, "but one day they passed me in the hall, and they, and they—"

"Go on," Mrs. Parks said gently. "What happened?"

"They growled at me," Melissa said quickly, as if she was embarrassed.

The rest of the class started to laugh, but one look from Mrs. Parks silenced them. "That frightened you?" Mrs. Parks asked quietly. Melissa nodded, head down.

"They pushed me against the lockers when they passed me in the hall," Delia offered next. "I don't like feeling scared and I don't like people who are rude."

"You bring up an important point, Delia," Mrs. Parks said. "Rather than talk about any specific people, let's talk about fear and aggression and what it does to us. If you look at events in our history book, you'll see that wars have sometimes started simply because of some folks who were too aggressive and others who were too fearful. Look at what Hitler did," she offered.

"So we gonna have a war here at school?" asked Aziz, the tallest boy in the eighth grade.

"Of course not," Mrs. Parks assured the class. "But if we understand what causes problems, perhaps we can work to fix them before the situation gets out of hand."

"So what do we do?" Delia asked.

"Has anybody ever talked to the Tollivers, tried to make friends with them?" asked Jesse, who had transferred to the school shortly after the twins.

"No way, man!" Aziz told him. "You want to get iced?"

"Wait. Jesse has a good point," Mrs. Parks insisted. "Sometimes the best way to destroy an enemy is by making friends with him. It's probably very hard to transfer into a school when the school year has already started."

"You got that right!" said Jesse. "But everyone was really straight-up with me, helped me find my way around school, told me what teachers were stupid and which were cool—they told me you were one of the cool ones, Mrs. Parks," he added with a grin. Mrs. Parks rolled her eyes and called on Aziz again, who was waving his hand wildly.

"Yeah, but Jesse came in here without an attitude. Nobody was scared of him from day one," Aziz reminded the class.

"We keep going back to the idea of fear," Mrs. Parks commented. "From what I can see, all of you are excited about being afraid. It's like it's the cool thing to do. I've known people to be frightened of me when they see me in an elevator!" The class chuckled.

"If I hadn't done my homework and I saw you in an elevator, I guess I'd be scared too!" joked Quinn, a boy who rarely did his homework on time.

Mrs. Parks laughed and told him, "Anytime YOU see me, Quinn, you'd better be afraid, because one of these days I'm going to show up at your house, right around dinnertime, and ask your mother why you can't remember your homework!"

Quinn jumped from his seat and fell on his knees. "Oh, please! Not the visit-your-mama-at-dinner torture! Anything but that! I promise I'll be good!"

"Get up, Quinn," Mrs. Parks said, laughing, "which reminds me—class, get out your homework."

Everybody groaned as they dug for their papers, but it seemed to Delia that everyone felt better because Mrs. Parks had loosened a bit of the tension they all felt. Quinn, of course, didn't have his homework, but Delia was glad that the attention was on him. She had not done her homework either. It was a reading assignment on Egyptian culture, along with several questions to answer. Delia figured that she could learn as much as she needed by listening in class, and would make up for the missed homework grade by offering to do an extra project—maybe a model of a pyramid or a mummy. But most of the class period had been taken up with the discussion of the Tolliver problem. Mrs. Parks had time only for a brief discussion of Egypt before the bell rang. The homework was to read the next chapter. She might never get the class help she needed to fake it on the test. Delia sighed as she walked down the steps to English, where she saw Yolanda just closing her locker.

"You ready for English?" Yolanda asked her as they pushed their way slowly through the crowded hall.

"Yeah, I guess. Hey, Yo Yo, are *you* scared of the Tollivers? You make a joke out of everything." They were standing outside of the classroom door.

"Not really," Yolanda replied. "I think this whole thing will blow over. I remember when me and my parents were living in Africa and a roving band of tigers had us cornered and all we had were the pencils from the mission school to fight them with."

"Yolanda!" Delia interrupted with a laugh. "Tigers come from Asia, not Africa, and you never were there, anyway!"

"It might have been a dream," Yolanda replied with a grin, "but it seemed very real. It's not a lie if you really believe it, is it?"

"Sometimes it's hard to tell the difference between the truth and a lie," Delia mused. "And it doesn't really matter who believes it."

seven

YOLANDA BOUNDED INTO THE CLASSROOM, BUT DELIA hesitated a moment outside the door of her English class. The Tollivers, even though they said very little, seemed to dominate the spirit of every class she shared with them. Delia took a deep breath, walked in, and headed to the cluster of chairs where her group sat. The class had been divided for something Miss Benson called "cooperative learning groups." Delia figured it was something her teacher had learned in a college education class, but Delia liked working in groups because it was easy to hide her problem. They had been allowed to pick their own group members this time, but sometimes Miss Benson assigned people so the kids wouldn't always work with their friends. Delia figured Miss Benson let them pick their own for this project so she wouldn't have to deal with the Tollivers. Nobody had chosen them to be in their group, which seemed to please everybody. They worked together in the back of the room, talking to each other with their books closed. They acted as if the rest of the class did not exist.

Miss Benson walked around to each group, offering suggestions and comments, sometimes making little jokes. When she got to the Tollivers, she simply said, "The group project reports are due next week." They ignored her as if she were an insect buzzing near them. She walked over to Delia's group, which included Randy, Yolanda, and Jesse. "How's it going here?" she asked cheerfully. "Any problems?"

Delia had watched the video of *Lord of the Flies* after she got home from Double Dutch practice, so she basically knew the story. But she also knew from experience that moviemakers often changed characters and even major events in a book just to make the movie more interesting. So she listened carefully to the other students in the group, comparing what she had heard about the first few chapters they had read with what she had seen in the video at home. So far, they seemed pretty similar.

"So you got a bunch of schoolboys stranded on a desert island. How fake is that?" Randy was asking. "There's no such thing as a desert island anymore. There's people everywhere on this planet!"

"This book was written a long time ago," Yolanda said. "Back then there were lots of available islands! My grandfather discovered the last desert island, you know. It was just before I was born, on one of his explorations of the Pacific Ocean."

"Here she goes again, Miss Benson," Randy complained with a laugh.

Miss Benson wisely chose not to deal with the tale of Yolanda's grandfather. Instead she asked, "Jesse, do you think that boys that age—nine, ten, eleven—could survive without adults?"

Jesse shifted in his seat. "I doubt it. I've got a little brother who's nine, and I think his brain cells are made out of oatmeal. He got lost in the mall last week. But then, if the desert island had a food court and a McDonald's, maybe he'd survive. That's how he found his way out of the mall."

"I don't think this island had food courts," Randy said, laughing. "I read the whole book already. These kids were into more gruesome stuff, like killing and eating pigs."

"What would you do if you were all alone, Randy?" Delia asked quietly.

The smile faded from Randy's face. "I'd do just fine," he said quickly. "I know how to take care of myself." He turned his attention to his book bag on the floor, and began rummaging through it.

"I'd be scared," Delia admitted. "My mom gets on my nerves sometimes, but I need her."

"All I need to survive is electricity for my hair curlers and television and stereo, and a bag of money, and I'd be just fine!" Yolanda asserted, while grinning at Jesse. "When we lived in London, I lived alone for six months while my parents worked as missionaries in the outback of Australia. I was the same age as the kids in this book."

"For real?" asked Jesse, who was new enough not to know about Yolanda's history of colorful storytelling.

"Yeah, for real," she replied with a look of innocence on her face. "And I did NOT become a savage like the kids in this story. Civilized folks don't do that."

"Yolanda, you think 'civilized' means hot tubs and helicopters. 'Civilized' has something to do with how folks treat each other. Right, Miss Benson?" Randy asked.

Miss Benson smiled with relief that at least one student seemed to be getting the idea. "Good point, Randy," she said with encouragement.

Randy nodded at the teacher, then turned back to

Yolanda to blast her. "Besides, Yo Yo, you've never even been to London! And you ain't got sense enough to live alone!" Yolanda ignored him and got her mirror and lipstick and brush out of her book bag. "You gotta watch Yo Yo," he told Jesse. "Believe only half of what she says—maybe even less." Jesse didn't seem to care, Delia thought. He was busy watching Yolanda brush her long black hair.

Miss Benson tried to redirect their discussion. "Without adults," she began, "the children in this book turn to fear and violence. Jack and his hunters take over."

"See, Yolanda!" Randy said gleefully. "One of these days you're gonna go too far! Gonna have us all hunting each other!"

Yolanda turned her chair so her back faced Randy. She pretended she had not heard him. Jesse laughed and looked at Yolanda with eyes of admiration. Delia said nothing, but listened carefully and remembered everything.

Jesse announced with authority, "Seems to me that things got really bad for them 'cause they couldn't figure out what was true and what was just a nightmare. Bunch of little kids running around so scared, they got things really messed up. Seems dumb to me."

Miss Benson sighed and tried once more to get the group back on track. "Here's an idea for your group project," she suggested. "Why don't you do something on truth and fear? Use ideas from the novel, but make it apply to the world we live in today."

Jesse raised his hand. "Miss Benson, I know what we can do. How about if we do a skit on modern-day fears and lies?"

Delia immediately liked Jesse's idea. It would be fun,

easy, and involved no reading. "And I'll draw a poster to go along with it," she volunteered.

"And I'll do one on lies," Yolanda said with a grin.

"Good choice," Randy teased.

"This sounds wonderful," Miss Benson said. "Get busy." She moved on to the next group, who wanted to make their project a quiz show using questions about the book, and the next group, who wanted to bring squirt guns to class to demonstrate violence. That one she rejected—loudly and emphatically. Delia noticed that she never did get back to the Tollivers to ask them what type of project they would do.

eight

THAT EVENING AT DOUBLE DUTCH PRACTICE YOLANDA AND Delia sat on the sidelines, waiting their turn while the Little Bees jumped. Charlene and Misty sat on a bench behind them. It was hot in the gym, but Yolanda had on a heavy warm-up with a hood.

"Why you dressed like that, girl?" Delia asked.

"I saw on TV last night that satellites out in space can see everything you do. I'm dressed in disguise just in case somebody from another country is planning to steal my moves as I jump. I'm a national treasure, you know."

"You're a trip, Yo Yo." Delia laughed as she tied the laces on her tennis shoes.

"That's your life story, Yo Yo," Charlene added. "I'll never forget that time in sixth grade when you made that substitute think you were dying. Ketchup all on your clothes. Looked real for a minute." Charlene laughed, remembering the look on the substitute's face when she saw what she thought was blood.

Yolanda cracked up and screeched in a voice imitating the unfortunate sub, "Oh, my STARS!" Yolanda laughed so hard, she had to bend over. "Then she fainted, poor dear. The principal had to call the life squad. That was TOO funny!"

"That was cold, Yo Yo," Charlene said, still laughing. "That woman never came back after that day."

"It wasn't my fault!" Yolanda said. "The woman couldn't handle kids. I probably saved her life!"

"Double Dutch saved my life," Misty said quietly.

"How you mean?" Yolanda asked, her laughter stilled by Misty's voice. She pushed back the hood of her jacket and turned to face Misty.

"Nothing," Misty replied, suddenly embarrassed. But as the girls continued to stare at her, she went on. "It's just that Double Dutch is always there for me—my daddy's dead, my mama isn't able to work since she was in that car accident, and I got four little sisters to look out for, but Double Dutch gives me something to hold on to. Something good. I used to get really bad grades, but now, since I gotta have good grades to stay on the team, I got a reason to keep going." She bent down to tie her shoes, her cheeks flushed.

"I feel ya," Delia said, nodding her head, sensing Misty's discomfort. "Double Dutch even got me a good grade once in a class in school."

"Yeah," continued Yolanda. "Last year in social studies, when we had to do a stupid project on American cultural practices, me and Delia and Charlene did a class presentation on Double Dutch."

"Talk about an easy A!" Delia chuckled. "Ooh! That was dynamite! I wish all school projects were so much fun."

Charlene laughed. "Yeah, I remember that backwards flip you did into the ropes, Yolanda. You coulda broke your neck, doin' that fancy jump in that small space."

"Yeah, but she didn't," Delia reminded Charlene. "I

gotta give her credit—the girl is good. You looked like sliced ice that day—really slick, Yo Yo."

"I always look good when I flip," said Yolanda, who had removed her heavy jacket. "I still have the written report. I think I'll save it so I can use it again. I did a report on snakes in fifth grade. I've used it, with a few improvements, every year since then in science class. The teachers never know."

"Isn't that cheating?" asked Delia.

"Look who's talkin'," Yolanda replied with a sharp glance at Delia.

"I don't need no written report—I got it memorized," Delia said, glancing at Yolanda.

"You do not!" Misty challenged. "Dollar bet says you can't recite all that stuff."

"I have a photographic memory, dah-ling," Delia said with a voice like a movie star. "Make your bet a pizza and you're on!" She grinned at Charlene and Yo Yo.

"You got it! I don't believe you can do it!"

"You better hope Bomani gets here soon, Misty. Delia can memorize anything," Yolanda warned. Misty ignored her and waited for Delia to begin.

Delia grinned and took a deep breath. She spoke like a newscaster reading the news. "'Double Dutch is a jump rope sport that involves two rope turners turning two ropes in an eggbeater motion around one or two jumpers. Double Dutch requires an intricate display of skill, agility, and strength. It encourages creativity, teamwork, and sportsmanship, and develops physical fitness and mental discipline.'"

Charlene and Yolanda were rolling on the floor. Misty

stood with her mouth agape as Delia continued in her news reporter voice, this time holding her nose to make her voice sound artificial.

"'The sport,'" she continued, now prancing down the sidelines, "'believed to have originated with ancient Egyptian, Phoenician, and Chinese rope makers, has grown in popularity as a competitive sport. The American Double Dutch League was officially organized in nineteen seventy-three by two New York City police detectives.' Cops! Can you believe it?" she added in amazement.

Returning to her fake newscaster's voice, she continued. "'On Valentine's Day in nineteen seventy-four, the first Double Dutch tournament was held in New York City. Almost nine hundred children competed. Today in the U.S. more than one hundred thousand athletes nationwide and in foreign countries participate in Double Dutch programs for the chance to compete in the World Invitational Championships for honor and for scholarships.'" Delia paused, took her hand off her nose, and took a deep breath. "Want more?" she asked, laughing.

Yolanda said, "I told you so!"

Misty laughed and said, "You win! How do you remember all that stuff?"

Delia's smile faded. "Just smart, I guess. I don't know. Stuff just sticks." She sighed. Why was she so smart in some ways and so dumb in others?

Bomani arrived, as large and cheerful as ever, and announced, "Jumpers, are you ready? Let's begin this practice! Break into three groups. Group One—in the front of the gym. You know the routine. Everybody hop to it! Let me hear you shout it out!"

The gym echoed with the chants of three dozen jumpers as they began the first compulsory jumps.

> "*One-TWO*
> *One-TWO/Three-FOUR!/Five-SIX/Seven-*
> *EIGHT*
> *One-TWO.*"

Bomani then cried, "Okay! Let's try a couple of speed tests, jumpers! Two minutes on the clock, Randy. Little ones, take your time. Accuracy is as important as speed. Remember, you get ten points taken off your jump score every time you miss, so take your time and concentrate. Ready, Little Bees? Ready, Junior Bees? Ready, my Queen Bees?" They all signaled that they were ready. "Randy, hit it!" The gym resounded with the sounds of dozens of synchronized tapping feet.

Bomani gave them all a short break, then regrouped everyone into practice teams so they could work on individual skills for the various events. He walked over to Delia and the Queen Bees. "Let's work on the doubles freestyle first tonight, ladies. That's going to be key at the state meet. Misty, Charlene? Are you ready?"

As Delia and Yolanda turned the ropes while Misty and Charlene did the doubles routine, Delia watched Misty closely and admired her even more. *Nothing is really as it seems,* she thought as the ropes twisted in her hands.

After two hours of drills, timed practices, and jumping techniques, Bomani blew his whistle and told them all to take a break, get some water, and come back for a short team meeting. He gave Randy two stacks of typed sheets to pass out—one with information about the state and national tournaments that were coming up soon, as well as information about practices and local competitions for the next month. The other sheet concerned the new eligibility rules for eighth-grade Double Dutch competitors. Delia glanced at them, carelessly stuffed them into her gym bag, and began to stretch her legs while Bomani went over the highlights of the information on the sheets. The younger girls asked a million silly questions, but Bomani was patient and answered every one.

"Will they have bathrooms at the other gym?"

"Yes, DeLisa. They have very nice bathrooms at that gym."

"Do we take our ropes, or do we have to use their tricky ropes, like the ones that made me fall last time?"

"I'm sure it was that rope's fault that you fell, Shantelle. We'll take our own ropes just to make sure you come in first place." Bomani chuckled, then looked directly at Delia, Yolanda, Misty, and Charlene. His smile faded. "If you have read the green sheet Randy just handed you," he began, "you can see that the school board and the state Double Dutch association have agreed that all eighth-grade jumpers must pass the proficiency tests in order to continue their eligibility for ninth grade. I'm sure that will be no problem, because I know all of you are good students. I just wanted to let you know it's official."

Delia felt her breath catch in her chest.

Yolanda touched her gently. "It will be okay, Delia. We'll figure something out." The rest of the girls were packing up and getting ready to go home.

"I'm dumb as a rock," Delia said to the floor.

"Quit talking like that!" Yolanda fired back. "You always get good grades on projects and stuff."

"That's 'cause I always volunteer to do oral reports or art displays or science experiments while everybody else looks up stuff in the encyclopedia," Delia explained glumly.

"You do pretty well on tests, too," Yolanda continued. "Even math."

"That's 'cause I'm the best guesser in the world! Math is no problem as long as it's only numbers. But the word problems? Forget it! I just skip them and hope I've got enough right on the other parts to get by."

Yolanda thought out loud, "I wonder why doing numbers and figuring math out is easy for you, but reading words is so hard."

"My brain is fried. That's why," Delia replied morosely.

"It is not! Don't talk about yourself like that," Yolanda said sharply. "But what are you going to do about the stupid state test? Part of it is reading, and part of it is essay. Only a small part is multiple choice."

"I don't know. Mostly I write teeny-tiny, with a ballpoint pen that's almost out of ink. It's just about impossible to read, and most teachers give up after a while and pass me 'cause I'm nice in class. I'm sure they don't try to read it. But I can't pull that kind of stuff on the graders for the state test. I sure can't fool them with an oral report on the movie version of a book."

"Not likely."

"And if I fail the state test—"

"You fail eighth grade," Yolanda continued for her, her voice sounding pained. "And if you fail eighth grade—"

"Everybody will think I'm stupid. And everybody will find out I can't read."

"Even worse—"

"I won't be allowed to be in Double Dutch anymore!"

"And if you can't jump—"

"I'll just die!" Delia sighed as she stuffed her towel and water bottle into her gym bag. "My mom's here. I'll talk to you tomorrow, Yo Yo."

Yolanda, for once, had nothing to say. "Peace," she called quietly as Delia headed toward the door.

nine

RANDY DRAGGED INTO HIS HOUSE, TIRED AND HUNGRY. HE looked around hopefully, but nothing had changed. No duffel bag on the floor and no smell of his dad's spaghetti bubbling on the stove. Randy was so disappointed, he felt ill. He was sick of thinking about the Tollivers, sick of homework assignments, and sick of coming home to an empty house.

"Where are you, Dad?" Randy said to the walls. "And why haven't you called?" He threw himself on the sofa but did not turn on the television this time. "No telling who I'll see on there," he muttered.

The cat jumped on the sofa, looking for bologna or whatever leftovers Randy might offer, but seeing nothing, she curled up on Randy's chest and looked at him with bright, unblinking eyes.

As the cat purred on his chest, Randy stroked her back and sighed as he thought about his situation. His money was getting tight. His dad had given him fifty dollars when he left, and reminded Randy about the four hundred dollars they kept hidden in the shoe box in the bottom of the closet for emergencies. Randy couldn't believe that the rent and the phone bill had eaten up most of the money already, and he knew he didn't have enough left to pay the electric bill. At least the days were getting longer.

The cat made a small, careless mewing sound.

Randy did some quick calculations and figured he had enough for one more trip to the grocery store. "We may have to cut back on cat food," he said, grinning, as he rubbed the cat's head.

The cat stirred as if she understood. Randy sighed again as he tried to fight the clammy feeling of fear that crept over him. He couldn't stop thinking that something was wrong—really wrong. His father hadn't called in over a month. He always kept his cell phone on, but when Randy called, all he heard were dull, continuous, unanswered rings.

Randy kept hoping every day he came home, he'd find his dad sitting on the sofa, but instead he was greeted each day by the silent walls. He'd never been gone this long before. Randy knew he probably ought to call the police, but he was afraid that might get his dad in trouble for leaving Randy by himself. And what if they put him in foster care? That's what happened to kids who were left alone, but Randy had no intention of being treated like a kid. He could take care of himself.

His dad had always told him to trust his instincts. But right now he didn't even know what his instincts were, except that he was scared.

He shifted his weight on the sofa, and the cat jumped off Randy's chest to the coffee table. "Where is he, Cat?"

At that moment the phone rang, startling Randy. He jumped to reach for it while the cat leaped deftly to the floor, annoyed at the sudden movement. "Dad?" Randy said hopefully.

Delia's laughter sparkled softly on the line. "Sorry,

Randy, it's just me. You're expecting a call from your dad?"

"Yeah. He'll probably call tonight, though. What's up?"

"I just called to see what you wanted to do about that English project. You got any ideas?"

"Nah, not yet. How about you?"

"I got a couple of things rolling around in my head. Maybe we can . . . hey, my mom is calling me to go to the grocery store with her, so can I call you later tonight?"

"Sure thing. After I eat, my brain works better, anyway. Catch you later."

"Bye."

Randy hung up the phone. *I sure wish I coulda asked her to bring me stuff from the grocery store,* he thought as he opened the last can of cat food. The cat, fully absorbed in the turning can and the smell coming from it, nearly knocked it out of Randy's hand as he placed it on the floor. "I guess I'd better go to the store myself," he decided. He stuffed the last of the money into his coat pocket and headed down the street to the corner market.

Prices were higher there than at the big supermarket near the mall, but this was quick and easy. Even though he shopped slowly and carefully, and checked prices on every box and can, Randy knew that the small assortment of food in his cart was all he could afford. He sighed as he unpacked the cart and watched the electronic scanner register the price of each item. He paid for his groceries, counted the money very carefully, and double-checked his change. He had put back a couple of boxes of cereal and a six-pack of soda at the last minute so he wouldn't be completely broke. In his pocket, he had seventeen dollars left—no more hidden emergency money. Just seventeen dollars. And all of the groceries fit into two brown bags.

When he got home, he fixed himself a can of soup and three hot dogs. It was filling, but he knew he'd be hungry again before he went to bed. *Dad will come home soon,* he told himself. *Then we'll go out to dinner and get us two of the biggest steaks on the menu—maybe even three—one for the cat!*

He called Delia then, hoping he would hear the little interrupting beeping sound that indicated there was another call on the line, a call from his dad. Delia sounded glad to hear from him. "You finish dinner?" he asked.

"Yeah, me and my mom were both hungry when we shopped, so we got all kinds of goodies that she usually doesn't buy. We had a huge dinner and even a pie for dessert."

"Sounds great," Randy said with a little envy.

"Did you hear from your dad yet?" Delia asked.

Randy hesitated and considered telling her everything, but he could see nothing but trouble if he did. Besides, he had enough food to last for another week or so, if he was careful. And he was sure his dad would be back before then. So he said, "Uh, yeah, he did. I talked to him just a few minutes ago. He'll be home soon."

"That's good. Randy, if you ever need anything, you know you can call me. You told me the other day that you'd protect me from the Tollivers, and I appreciate that. I doubt if I can be much protection to you, as big as you are, but you just understand you can call me if things get rough. You got that?" Randy could hear Delia let out a deep breath.

"I gotcha," Randy replied softly. He didn't want Delia to

know how much her offer meant to him, so he changed the subject as well as his tone. "Now, what are we gonna do about this stupid English project?"

"Well, in class we talked about a skit. I thought we could do something that shows how fear can take over a school, you know, like one of those schools they show on the TV specials."

"Sounds a little too real," Randy said, sighing. "Everybody at school is so jumpy. Maybe we should do something funny instead," he suggested.

"Good idea. How about if everybody at school believes they're about to be invaded by Martians?"

"We can ask Yolanda to do the research. She's probably been to Mars three or four times!" Randy laughed.

"How about if the kids at this school in our skit are afraid of being taken to Mars to be dissected?" Delia offered.

"Yeah, and somebody says there are lists going around the school with names of kids who are about to be shipped out."

"Of course nobody has *seen* any list."

"For that matter, nobody has seen any Martians," Randy added. "It's all based on fear and rumors."

"I think this is gonna be good, Randy," Delia said. "It will be fun to do, too."

"I wonder what the Tollivers will do for their project," Randy mused.

"Something scary, I'm sure," Delia replied. "Hey, my other line is beeping. I gotta go. At least we got something to tell Miss Benson tomorrow. Catch you later."

Delia hung up, and Randy sat on the sofa in the silence

of the small apartment. His stomach growled a little, but he ignored it and stared at the phone, hoping it would ring once more with his dad on the other end. But the phone, like the rest of the apartment, was silent.

Randy leaned back then, trying not to think of what might have happened to his father, and dozed a little. The ringing of the phone startled him awake, and he sat up and grabbed the phone on the second ring.

"Hello?" Randy said hopefully into the receiver.

"Winston Youngblood, please," said a voice that was so artificial sounding, it might have been a computer.

"He's not available at the moment," Randy replied. "May I help you?"

"This is Miss Espy from the Cincinnati Gas and Electric Company. We were wondering if the payment for your heat and light has been made recently. We show the last payment was over six weeks ago."

Randy couldn't believe that a bill collector was calling this late in the evening. Then he figured that was the only time they could be sure to catch people. "I mailed that check yesterday," Randy lied smoothly. *I sound like Yolanda!* "You should have it tomorrow or the next day at the very latest," Randy added.

"I will make a note of that," the computer-sounding Miss Espy replied. *She has probably heard such lies many times before,* Randy thought. And she probably didn't believe him. But Randy didn't care. He had bought himself a little time, and his dad would probably be home by morning. At least he hoped so.

Randy finished his homework, turned off all the lights, and slid his large frame into bed. He listened to his alarm clock ticking and water dripping in the sink. The cat jumped onto the bed when Randy was almost asleep. She curled up into a tight ball at his feet. Randy didn't try to kick her off.

Randy fell asleep slowly. He thought of his dad and how close they had become. He tried not to let negative thoughts drift into his mind, but visions of his father hurt or bleeding or even dead kept slicing into the images in his mind. Randy pulled his covers up around his neck, but it didn't help. He was afraid.

ten

"How's Double Dutch practice coming, Delia?" her mother asked as they drove to school the next morning. "You've got practice after school tonight?"

Delia gathered her book bag, her gym bag, and a small overnight bag from the back seat of the car as her mother pulled into the school parking lot. "Practice is cool, Mom. We'll go to State for sure, probably even Nationals. You know we're bad!"

"I'm going to stop by and watch you again real soon," her mother promised. "Tomorrow is Saturday. For once, I don't have to work on the weekend."

"Stay home and rest, Mom," Delia said quickly. "You've seen us practice a million times. Put your feet up and enjoy an empty house for a little while. Dad will take me to Double Dutch after school and tomorrow, and you know he'll be there with Jillian. That always upsets you, and when you get bent outta shape, I can't jump well."

Delia's mom sighed. Delia glanced at her, knowing the sight of Delia's dad with his new wife still made her feel terrible. And she knew her mother was grateful to have a reason not to go to practice. Delia usually spent every other weekend with her father and Jillian. Delia didn't like it much, but she knew she had to make the effort. She loved her dad, tolerated her stepmother, and packed her travel bag every other weekend to keep everybody happy.

"I love you, Mom," Delia said as she kissed her mother on the cheek. She gathered her bags and got out of the car. "I'll call you tomorrow. See you Sunday!" She waved once more and headed up the walkway to the school.

"Hey, Yo Yo!" Delia called when she noticed Yolanda's bouncing ponytail a few feet in front of her. She was walking with Charlene.

Yolanda turned and waved. "You got enough bags, girl?" Charlene asked as Delia trudged up the sidewalk toward them.

"Book bag. Gym bag. Dad bag," Delia said as she shifted the bags onto her other shoulder.

"Oh, yeah. I forgot it was your daddy weekend. How's Miss Jillian?"

"She's okay. She doesn't hassle me, which is cool," Delia answered.

"Did you hear the latest?" Yolanda jumped with excitement.

"I just got here. What's up?" Delia asked.

"The Tollivers are planning something!" Yolanda replied in a hushed voice.

"Who says?" Charlene asked.

"Planning what? And how do you know?" Delia demanded.

"Something secret. Something big. Something terrible," Yolanda said slowly and with mystery in her voice. "I heard a girl on the bus say she read about it on a Web site."

"So what makes you think it's true?" Delia asked skeptically.

"Everything on the Web is true!" Yolanda asserted with conviction in her voice. "It's the new place for truth and information in the world!"

"Yeah, right," Charlene said sarcastically.

"Information, maybe. Truth? I doubt it," Delia said as they walked to their lockers. "Don't go spreading stuff unless you're sure, Yo Yo. I wouldn't want the Tollivers to find out you've been telling lies on them. Be careful what you say."

"She's right, Yolanda," Charlene added. "You don't want them mad at you."

"Then they ought to find that girl on the bus. She started it," Yolanda retorted. "I gotta get to the bathroom to put on some lipstick. Jesse is in my first-bell Spanish class, and I gotta look good! *Adiós!*" She headed down the hall, digging in her purse for her makeup as she walked. She didn't see the Tollivers as they turned the corner.

Delia saw the collision that was about to happen and cried out, "Yolanda! Look where you're going!" But she couldn't get the words out in time. Yolanda, who had just successfully pulled her lipstick out of her purse and opened it, looked up just in time to see the angry faces of the Tolliver brothers barreling toward her, demanding hall space as they always did. She had no time to jump out of the way, and the edge of her lipstick brushed across the back of Tabu's hand as they pushed by her. Tabu stopped abruptly and looked at the bright red stain on his pale brown skin. Titan turned and stopped as well, and both of them walked toward Yolanda as she backed toward the lockers, fear showing plainly on her face.

"You did that?" Tabu's words were both a question and

an accusation. He lifted his lipstick-marked hand and held it menacingly in front of her face. Delia, Charlene, and several other kids stood nearby, afraid to interfere, ready to run for help if necessary.

Instead of screaming, however, Yolanda took a deep breath and grinned like a cartoon cat. "Do you like the color?" she asked brightly. She spoke quickly and nervously. "We're doing an experiment for my home economics class—testing the colors of new lipsticks on the men of the school. Would you like to try another color?" Delia listened to her friend in amazement—she knew Yolanda was terrified, but she seemed to be faking it quite well.

Tabu said nothing but continued to stare at Yolanda as if she were a bug to be squashed. Then he did something completely unexpected. He smiled. "You got guts, girl." The smile disappeared in a second, and he and his brother turned and continued with their usual fierce look and determined stride down the hall.

Yolanda slid down the lockers and onto the floor. "I thought I was gonna die!" she said between gasps of air and almost hysterical giggles. "That was not good for my weak heart. I think somebody should take me to the emergency room."

"We were about to call 911 and tell them to bring a mop to wipe what was left of you off the floor!" Delia teased as she helped Yolanda up. "Only you could talk your way out of a beating by the Tollivers!"

"Did you see him smile?" Yolanda asked with amazement.

"Fear got you seein' things, girl," Charlene said. "I don't think the Tollivers know how to smile."

"For real! He did! Just one quick little smile," Yolanda insisted.

"I saw it," Delia admitted quietly to Yolanda. "Maybe he was imagining what you'd look like in little pieces."

Most of the kids didn't believe Yolanda, but then, most kids never did. She headed on to class as the bell rang, shaking her head in amazement. She never did put on her lipstick.

Delia breezed through her math quiz in first bell, but she worried about her second-bell social studies class. Mrs. Parks had been giving lots of reading assignments for homework, with very little discussion in class the next day, to Delia's annoyance. And Yolanda wasn't in her class to help her.

Today an all-school assembly was scheduled. As soon as the bell rang, Quinn raised his hand. "We goin' to the assembly, Mrs. Parks?"

"Yes, Quinn. It's your lucky day. No class today. The principal has called this assembly, and it should take all bell." The whole class cheered.

"What's it about, Mrs. Parks?" asked Aziz.

"I'm going to sing and dance," Mrs. Parks teased him as she quickly took attendance. She quieted with a hand the laughing of the class, then told them seriously, "It's about safety. We want to make sure we have a safe end to the school year."

"Boring!" whispered Aziz. "I'd rather hear her sing!"

Delia figured this special assembly had been called to deal with the Tolliver situation. The whole school was nervous and edgy. As she filed into the noisy auditorium, she spotted Yolanda, who had managed to find a seat next to

Jesse. She didn't see Charlene, but she saw Randy, sitting near the front, laughing loudly with some of the boys from his gym class. The Tolliver twins sat quietly in the back.

The principal, Mr. Lazarro, was tall and thin and had a long, pale neck. The kids called him Lazarro the Lizard, but they liked him. He took the time to talk to them when he passed them in the hall, and if a kid got sent to his office for discipline, it was known that he would listen to all sides and try to be fair in his decisions.

He adjusted the microphone upward to match his height, and quieted the room full of students with just a clearing of his throat. "I have called this assembly today to discuss some very important issues with you, my young friends. We want to make sure you are safe here at school, and it is our job to find a way to make that happen. We will have a brief presentation by Officer Bobby Brown, then I'll let you ask questions. Bob? They're all yours."

The kids cheered. Officer Bob had been at the school for years and he knew most of the kids by name. He was the Cincinnati police officer assigned to all the junior high schools in the city. His job was to be more of a friend and a resource person for the students than an enforcer. However, when someone went over the line, like earlier in the year when a kid brought a knife to school and threatened a teacher, Officer Bob had taken him out of the building in handcuffs.

He approached the microphone, adjusted it downward, for he was much shorter than the principal, and got them quiet with just three words. "I hate funerals," he began. The auditorium was suddenly silent. "I have been to too many funerals of young people who had not learned to live and were certainly not ready to die. I have seen death from gun violence. I have seen death from car wrecks. And I've seen death from just plain stupidity. I don't want to see it anymore." He paused for effect. Delia sat up straight and listened.

"We are instituting some new policies here at the school. It is happening all over the country, so don't think you're being picked on, and don't think you're special. First of all, this weekend a metal detector will be installed at the front door." Everyone groaned. "Silence!" demanded Officer Bob. "Beginning on Monday, everyone must enter through this door and, just like at the airport, you'll pass through a simple detector that will make a noise if it picks up a metal object in your book bag or pocket. So don't put hubcaps in your book bag anymore," he added, trying to make them laugh. It didn't work.

"What if I got a metal belt buckle?" yelled Aziz from the middle of the auditorium.

"As loose as you wear your pants, Aziz," Officer Bob joked, "it probably means your pants are gonna fall down when we run your belt through the machine!" Everybody laughed this time. "Seriously," Officer Bob added, "as long as you're not carrying weapons or dangerous objects, you won't have a problem. Just like in the airport. Unfortunately, this kind of business is a part of our lives these days."

He sighed and continued. "We will also be instituting spot checks of lockers for drugs and alcohol. I know none of you has ever even heard of drugs and you'd faint if you tasted alcohol, but just in case we've got some drug-using, wine cooler–sipping aliens from Mars tiptoeing around here, we're going to check. Like I said, if you're clean, we've got no problems."

"You gonna check the teachers, too?" Delia recognized Randy's booming bass voice.

"Teachers have voluntarily offered to be included in the metal detector checks as well as the other spot checks, to make it very clear that we mean business," Officer Bob replied. "You didn't expect that, did you, Randy?"

Randy shrugged his shoulders. It really was a little surprising that the teachers would do that, Delia thought.

"We're in this together," Officer Bob continued. "One last thing," he added. "I'm assigned to this school only until the end of the school year, and I will be here all day every day. You can stop by anytime just to talk, to ask questions, or to report anything that looks suspicious or dangerous. It's a good way to stop the rumors that get started when kids get scared. I'm here for you. I want each and every one of you to remember that. This is the best school in Cincinnati, and we're going to keep it that way!" With that, he sat down. The students clapped enthusiastically.

Mr. Lazarro returned to the microphone then, making it squeak as he moved it up. "We have only a few minutes before the bell rings. I'm going to let you ask a few questions—but within these guidelines: no questions about specific students or specific situations. Those are the things that should be discussed privately with Officer Bob. Are there any general questions about the new procedures?"

Charlene raised her hand and asked, "Will parents have to go through the metal detectors?"

"You better keep yo daddy outta here, if that's the case!" yelled a boy from the other side of the auditorium.

Mr. Lazarro ignored the boy and told her, "Yes, Charlene. Everyone who comes into this building—the mailman, maintenance people, even the school superintendent—will be checked. It sure will make *me* feel safer, and I'm sure your parents will be glad as well. Each parent will receive a letter today explaining the new procedures." The bell rang then, and Mr. Lazarro dismissed them to their next-bell classes. Everyone had an opinion, and the auditorium and halls buzzed with conversation as the students digested the information.

Delia met up with Yolanda and Jesse in the main hall near the front doors. "Well, I guess this will be the prison entrance!" Yolanda said with gloom. "It's all those dumb Tollivers' fault. We had a perfectly nice school before they transferred here."

"I transferred here too," Jesse reminded her. "Don't blame the Tollivers for everything."

"Yeah, but you didn't go on national television and make threats that have got everybody scared. You don't walk down the hall like you got mud for blood."

"You ever see me bleed?" Jesse teased her, trying to make her laugh.

"No, and I hope I never do." Yolanda refused to be consoled. "I hate this—being scared all the time."

Delia touched her arm and said, "It's gonna be okay, Yo Yo. Let's get to class."

In English, Miss Benson let them work in groups again. The new rules and the nervous feelings of fear and uncertainty made the group discussions loud and edgy. Delia and Randy explained their idea about the Martians to Yolanda and Jesse, and Yolanda immediately volunteered to be the main Martian in the skit.

"Look, Yo Yo, you're missing the point. You can't be the

Martian in the skit, because there aren't any real aliens taking over the planet. Everybody just thinks it's about to happen," Delia explained.

Yolanda sniffed and played with her hair. "Real Martians would be more fun. Well, I'll be the one who starts the rumors."

"Now THAT's the right part for you," Randy said, laughing. Even Jesse had to agree.

Delia said, "I have an idea! How about if we videotape it? I could use my mom's camera. And we could film it at my house next week." Delia knew a videotaped project would earn a very good grade.

"Great idea!" Jesse said enthusiastically. "This is gonna be phat!"

"I'll write the script," Yolanda offered, "since everybody thinks I'm the expert on making up stories around here. But I'm not gonna do it all by myself."

"I'll help," Jesse declared quickly. "Can we get together this weekend?"

"We've got Double Dutch practice all day Saturday," Delia reminded them, "and I'm at my dad's house this weekend, so that's not a good idea."

"How about next week?" Yolanda suggested. "Tuesday. My house."

"You gonna have food?" Randy asked.

"We'll kill a couple of the cattle from our herd in our backyard and see if that's enough for you to start with."

"I can live with that," Randy said, grinning. Yolanda and Delia both gave him a smile of disgust.

Miss Benson walked around the room, checking the progress of each group. Delia glanced at her as she clearly saved the Tolliver twins for last. The Tollivers sat in the back, talking quietly. Tabu typed on a small laptop computer. Titan wrote in a notebook that was filled with pages and pages of neat blue script. The other students glanced nervously at them from time to time, but no one spoke to them.

The teacher took a deep breath and approached the two boys with a smile. "And how is your project coming, gentlemen? I appreciate the fact that you work so well together and that you are so well-behaved."

"You were expecting less?" Tabu asked without returning her smile.

"It is what I expect of all my students," retorted the teacher, who blushed a bit. "Have you decided what you will do for your project?"

"We're gonna do our project on the killings in *Lord of the Flies,*" Titan told her without looking up from his notebook.

"Is there anything else you can concentrate on? Something more positive?" Miss Benson asked hopefully.

Tabu glanced at her as if she were mud on his boot. "*You* picked the book. Why'd you give us a book to read that's got violence if you don't want to discuss it?"

"It's on the required reading list," Miss Benson answered lamely. "How, exactly, are you going to present this project?"

"It's gonna be a surprise," Titan answered. "You will never forget it."

The bell rang then, and the twins picked up their belongings and brushed past Miss Benson without another word.

eleven

THE NEXT COUPLE OF WEEKS WERE BUSY FOR ALL OF them, especially Randy, and for that he was glad. The Ohio State Double Dutch Championships were held on a Saturday in Columbus. Teams from all over Ohio, and a few from just across the river in Kentucky, met for the competition. It was just like the national finals in intensity, only smaller. The huge gym was filled with crisply ironed T-shirts, frantic practice jumps in the halls and parking lot, and the electric excitement of competition and challenge.

Randy could tell Bomani really appreciated the help as Randy had made sure everyone was accounted for in the bus to Columbus and at the gym. When they got there, it was Randy's job to help collect tickets at the door, pass out programs, and sell souvenirs. Later, he helped out as a timer, a scorekeeper, and a counter during the speed jumps. Randy ironed T-shirts, kept up with the third graders, and made sure everybody had lunch tickets. The high-school gym they used was noisy, crowded, and not air-conditioned, so it was Randy's job to make sure all the jumpers from Cincinnati had water. He made sure all the judges had pencils and plenty of score sheets. At the end of the day he was exhausted, but relieved to have been so busy. It kept his mind off his father.

Randy noticed there were a number of boys who were jumpers on the various teams from across the state. They were muscular, athletic, and always good crowd pleasers as they did their jumps, especially in the speed and freestyle events. He had considered jumping on a team a couple of years ago, but he liked his role now—the second in command in charge of whatever was needed. It made him feel useful.

Randy knew the procedure in his sleep—it was the same in all competitions: the singles compulsory, timed jumps, and freestyle, beginning with the youngest jumpers and continuing to the oldest competitors, followed by the doubles competitions. Sometimes the whole thing got on his nerves because it took all day, but he liked the tight feeling of anticipation that grabbed him every time the jumpers on their team picked up the ropes. Everybody felt it as they waited their turn to be called, nervously watching the others and cheering for those who did outstanding performances.

At last, the call was made for eighth-grade singles freestyle jumpers. Delia, Charlene, and Yolanda walked like professionals to their places, heads held high, absolute confidence on their faces. Delia glanced at Randy just before the buzzer sounded, and grinned.

They completed their routine with gymnastic twists and elastic leaps. At one point, Yolanda, who was turning, tossed her end of the rope to Charlene, who grabbed it while she was still jumping, and in one turn of the ropes, Charlene moved effortlessly from jumper to turner, the rhythm of the ropes never stopping. Delia then tossed her end and completed the same move, so that each person had changed positions, but the ropes never faltered.

"Beauty in motion," Randy whispered, shaking his head. Yolanda, Delia, and Charlene completed the routine perfectly, ending with the three of them doing a jumping bow in perfect synchronization before the judges' table. The whole routine got a standing ovation from the crowd. Bomani cheered with approval, even though he was not really supposed to.

When the results were tallied at the end of the very long day, the Queen Bees, the Junior Bees, and the Little Bees all scored well and got selected to go on to the national finals—called "world championships" because the teams from several countries competed as well. Delia and her group had scored exceptionally high, with their singles freestyle taking them over the top.

The following week, the busy schedule showed no signs of slowing. Double Dutch practice was now every day after school, in preparation for the upcoming world championships. Randy and the rest of his group from English class had met at Yolanda's house, where they wrote the script, and they all had gone to Delia's house several times, where they videotaped sections of their skit.

Randy was glad he had so much to do. It made the silent, lonely nights at home easier to bear. His food supply had just about disappeared once more. A little peanut butter. Some cheese. No cat food. He got free lunch at school, there were usually snacks available after Double Dutch practice, and he enjoyed working on the English project with Yolanda and Delia because they ordered pizza or one of their mothers would fix them something to eat.

But by the following Saturday, Randy had come to the end of all his money and all the food he had in the house.

He knew what he had to do. He sighed, looked at the VCR under the television, and unplugged it. The cat looked at him curiously as he wrapped the cord around the VCR and headed slowly for the door. He remembered when they had gotten the VCR. It was the best Christmas they'd ever had.

He opened the door of Clifford's Pawn Shop around the corner and set the VCR on the counter. Mr. Clifford, a skinny, wrinkled man with a cigar stuck in one corner of his mouth and glasses perched on the end of his nose, eyed Randy suspiciously. "This is not stolen," Randy began as he walked toward the counter. "I shouldn't have to explain myself, but I guess you get all kinds in here. This belongs to me and my father, and I need some money. My dad is . . . uh . . . sick, and we're short on cash. How much can I get for this?"

The old man said nothing at first. He looked at Randy with narrowed eyes, staring intently through the purple-rimmed glasses on his nose, apparently evaluating the situation. "How much you need?" he finally asked.

"Huh?" Randy was a little surprised. "I thought you offered me what you think it's worth."

"If I did that, I'd give you about fifteen dollars," replied the owner. "How much you need?" he repeated.

Randy thought for a minute. "Fifty dollars will hold me—I mean us—for a little while. I'll give the folks at the electric company twenty dollars, and I'll keep the rest for food."

"Your daddy on drugs?" the owner asked.

"What? No, sir! I told you my father is sick. Really sick." Randy bowed his head and sighed. He felt sick himself at that moment. He was tired of being alone, tired of making do, tired of pretending that everything was all right when nothing could be further from the truth.

"I know your daddy. Winston Youngblood. You look just like him." Mr. Clifford kept staring at Randy. "Ain't seen him around here lately."

Randy's head jerked up. "You know my daddy? How?"

"Seen him around the neighborhood. He don't come in here much, but I know who he is. Is everything okay, son?" Mr. Clifford's eyes softened a bit. His voice seemed to offer understanding.

Randy was about to cry. He missed his dad so much. "Yeah, everything's fine," he forced himself to say. "Dad's just been sick. He can't work, and I'm trying to help out. That's all."

Mr. Clifford took the VCR and put it behind the counter. He continued to look at Randy very closely. "Giving the electric company twenty dollars is like spittin' in the ocean. Won't do much good," he said finally.

Randy sighed again. "I know. But last night when she called me for the fourth or fifth time, the lady from the electric company told me if I gave them a small payment she'd keep the lights on for another two weeks. I'm sure my dad will be better by then," Randy told him.

Mr. Clifford said nothing but turned to the cash register and took out some cash. He gave Randy a pink form. "Fill this out for me. Don't leave nothin' blank."

Randy obeyed, trembling a little from nervousness and a little from hunger. He had eighty-seven cents in his pocket.

Mr. Clifford took the form, looked at it carefully, and tossed it into a shoe box on the counter. "I have examined this VCR very closely," he said, although Randy knew he had only glanced at it, "and I find it to be rather valuable—a collector's item. Since I am a businessman, I cannot give you the full value, but I am willing to give you half of what I think it is worth."

"Seven dollars and fifty cents?" Randy asked hopelessly.

Mr. Clifford ignored him and said sternly, "You may not be aware of this, but your machine is worth over six hundred dollars!"

"Really?" Randy asked with astonishment. He knew for a fact that his father had bought it on sale at Wal-Mart for eighty dollars.

"Never doubt a man of business," Mr. Clifford said, softening his tone a bit. He handed Randy three crisp one hundred–dollar bills. "And don't go advertising to the neighborhood that I cheated you out of a valuable piece of merchandise!"

Randy looked at the money in disbelief. He could hold the tears back no longer. "Thank you, Mr. Clifford," he said softly. "Thank you so much."

Mr. Clifford peered at Randy once more through those purple spectacles. "Give the folks at the electric company fifty dollars, son, give thirty to the phone company, a hundred toward your rent, then space the rest out as best you can. Come see me if your dad gets better. And come see me if he don't. You hear?"

"Yes, sir," Randy mumbled.

"And don't be expectin' your TV to be no collector's item in a month or so. If things don't get better, you go get some help. Got that?"

"Yes, sir," Randy said again. "I really appreciate this."

"Get outta here now!" Mr. Clifford turned his back to Randy, pretending to sort through some papers on the counter.

Randy walked slowly toward the door of the shop. "Thanks again," he said quietly. "I'll be back." As Randy walked into the Saturday morning April sunshine, he sighed with relief, but he knew that he could not keep up this situation much longer. Along with food and other expenses, he knew that even Mr. Clifford's generosity would not last long. He evaluated all his options as he rode the bus downtown to the electric company.

As Mr. Clifford had predicted, the fifty dollars was enough to hold the lights on for another month at most. Randy left there and walked slowly across the busy downtown street to pay the phone bill, at least a small part of it. Finally, he stopped at a market and bought a few groceries, and headed home to feed the cat. He made himself a fat, juicy hamburger and ate it in three huge bites. He burped.

He plopped down on the sofa after eating, and found himself talking to the cat once more.

"Well, Cat, I gotta get help. I guess Dad has deserted me just like Momma did."

The cat, content and full for a change, dozed near his feet.

Randy mused, trying to figure out his limited options. His dad was an only child. His mother had been an only child. His grandparents were dead. He refused to call the police or a child abuse hotline. But he didn't know who else to call. A teacher? Too complicated. Bomani? He already had ten kids of his own. He had enough problems. Randy just didn't know what to do.

Randy stared at the phone. "Please call, Dad. I won't be mad. Just come home."

The phone, as if it had heard him, rang shrilly. Randy lunged to pick it up. "Hello," he said hopefully.

"Hi, Randy." Even Delia's cheerful voice didn't cheer Randy.

"Hey, Delia. What's up?"

"Not you. You sound down—like you're livin' in a pit or something."

"Actually, it's been a pretty good day," Randy told her. "I was just thinking about getting ready for practice. Starts at five, right?"

"Well, that's one reason why I called. Bomani's wife called, and four of their kids have the chicken pox, so he's canceling practice today."

"Great. I mean, I'm not glad his kids are sick, but I didn't feel like the noise and funk of practice today. I got a lot on my mind."

"Me, too," Delia said with a sigh. "You know that the state test is the week after we do our projects."

"Why do you care about that? I hear it's pretty easy."

"I don't like any kind of test. And I don't do good on standardized tests—all those little blue bubbles to fill in and somebody walking down the aisles looking over your shoulder, holding on to a stopwatch—freaks me out."

"Yeah, I feel ya. But you'll do fine. You're smart, Delia. Look what a good job you did filming us for Miss Benson's project."

"That was no test—that was fun! I bet we get an A on it."

"You got that right. Hey, Delia, what do you think the Tollivers are going to do for their project?"

"I have no idea. Miss Benson tried to get them to tell her, but they just told her wait and see."

"I think Miss Benson gave the assignment before she had it all figured out. An older teacher would have made us write down what we were going to do, then approved it. Miss Benson is fun, but she's kinda dumb as a teacher," Randy said.

"I don't think she's dumb—she just doesn't know all the teacher secrets yet."

Randy thought about his own secret that everyone was unaware of.

"When do the Tollivers give their presentation?" Delia asked.

"Let's see. We do ours on Tuesday. If we finish it in time, the Tollivers would do their presentation right after us. Ought to be an interesting day."

"Yeah, I don't know whether to be scared or worried," Delia said.

"Probably both." Randy laughed nervously.

"How's your dad?" Delia asked.

"Uh, he's good. Just left last night on another trip." Randy just couldn't bring himself to admit that his father had deserted him.

"How do you manage, Randy? Being by yourself all the time. Don't you get scared? Or lonely?"

"Naw, I like being alone. No one to mess with me. No one to beat me to the bathroom. I feel like I'm grown—livin' large—all on my own. It's great."

"Well, you got the large part down," Delia said with a laugh. "The rest is scary to me."

"I ain't never been scared," Randy lied as he imagined his father lying bleeding and dead on the side of the road, or, even worse, happily cooking spaghetti in a city hundreds of miles away, with no thoughts of Randy on his mind.

"Well, I have been, lots of times. The Tollivers scare me. Tests scare me. Thunderstorms freak me out. And being alone terrifies me. I'll catch you Monday. If you need to call me before then, I'll be at my dad's house. Later."

Delia hung up, and Randy stared at the phone, thinking about the day, about Delia, and about his dad. He thought about real fear and how it was slipping like smoke under his door, into his space, and throughout his body. He listened to the phone click, echo, then finally beep that annoying sound to let him know he needed to hang it up. He did so slowly, and the silence of the small apartment was somehow suddenly loud and stifling. Randy ran to his room, turned his radio up loud, and fell across his bed. The music bounced off his back as he buried his head in his pillow. He fell asleep with the music echoing through the empty rooms.

twelve

DOUBLE DUTCH PRACTICE ON MONDAY WAS HOT AND horrible. Delia tripped over the ropes like they were made of tree branches. She couldn't get past 50 on her speed jumps, when her average was usually closer to 350.

Randy yelled at her from across the floor, "Get it together, Delia. You jumpin' like a kindergartner—a clumsy one at that!"

"You're not the coach!" Delia yelled back at him. "Don't mess with me! At least I'm not sweatin' like a pig!"

Randy grabbed a towel and wiped his face. It had been unusually hot all day—more like July than April. Randy was hot and hungry and angry. "Well, you're jumpin' like a pig! We ain't gonna win nothin' if you jump like that at the finals next week!"

"I don't believe you're dissin' me like that!" she retorted angrily. "If you don't like it, you can just—"

"That's enough!" yelled Bomani from the other side of the gym. He was physically restraining two screaming, sweating ten-year-olds who were angry enough to fight. One swore she had been tripped. The other claimed she couldn't turn for somebody who was stupid and ugly. "Teammates do NOT fight each other," he told the girls sternly. "Go sit on the sidelines and make up, or I'm calling your parents to take you home. It is too hot to be dealin' with this kind of fool-ishness tonight." Both of them scowled, but they quieted down and obeyed. "And Delia," Bomani yelled, "Randy's right. Go get some water, rest a little, then try again. You're off your game tonight."

Delia stormed off the floor, hot with anger, as she dug in her bag for her water bottle. "How dare he talk to me like that?" she muttered to Yolanda. "Where's he get off thinkin' he can talk to me like he's my mama or something? He better fix his face to be lookin' someplace else!"

"It's the heat, Delia," Yolanda said, trying to calm her down. "You know Randy isn't usually like this. He's crazy about you—you know that."

"Well, he sure has a crazy way of showing it!" Delia was still angry. She refused to look at Randy, who sat near the table of refreshments that some parents had brought. "You jump for a while, Yo Yo. Get Charlene and Misty to turn for you. I'm not doing anybody any good."

"It's too hot for anything," Yolanda complained as she went to find her own water bottle. "When my body gets overheated, I sometimes go into cardiac arrest. I must be careful."

"You're gonna get arrested for tellin' tales," Delia said, chuckling. "Get out there and jump! Let me see your fastest speed routine."

Yolanda walked over to the ropes, gave the signal to Misty and Charlene, and proceeded to jump fast and furi-ous. She smirked when she stopped, and said to Delia, "Piece of cake!" The only signs that she was aware of the heat were small drops of perspiration on the bridge of her nose. Delia stood and cheered loudly. Yolanda, who clearly had been awesome, took a bow and walked off the gym floor. Bomani nodded in approval from the other side of the gym.

Randy set the timer for the younger girls, then moved slowly across the floor to the folding chair where Delia sat. She had her feet propped up on another chair and a wet paper towel on her forehead. Her eyes were closed.

"Hey, Delia, uh, my bad," Randy said softly. "I'm like, uh, sorry. You're the last person here who I want to be mad at me. I'm just . . . I'm just . . ." He could not finish the sentence.

Delia did not move or open her eyes at first. Finally she peeked from behind the quickly drying paper towel and asked, "What's wrong with you?"

Randy sighed. "Can I call you tonight? I've got something to tell you."

"What is it?" Delia asked, sitting up straight and looking at him intently. She could feel her anger melt.

"I promise I'll tell you tonight. I can't talk about it here. And Delia?" he added nervously.

"What?" she asked quietly.

"Don't mention this to Yolanda or Charlene. Please." Randy looked miserable.

Delia continued to look at him carefully. "Okay, no sweat." She smiled then. "Actually that's the problem—too much sweat tonight! But don't worry, I got your back."

Randy looked relieved as the buzzer for the timer sounded. He bounded back to the scoring table.

Yolanda, Misty, and Charlene headed directly for Delia when they finished their jumps. "What's up, girl? What did he say?"

"I thought you were supposed to be jumpin', not dippin' into somebody else's business!" Delia laughed.

"It's easy to do both," Yo Yo said between gulps as she swallowed half a bottle of water. "I do it all the time!"

"That's your problem!" Misty said. "If you'd concentrate on what we're supposed to be doing out there, instead of tryin' to run Delia's love life, we'd have the championship tied up!"

"Speak for yourself, girlfriend," Yo Yo replied. "I have no interest in Delia's love life. I have a dynamite love life of my own, thank you—seventeen boyfriends, last I counted—but it still might be interesting to hear what the large one has on his puny little mind."

"He was just talking about tomorrow's project presentation at school," Delia said smoothly.

"That wasn't a school project look he was giving you," Charlene said with envy in her voice. "That was a 'Hey-Delia-you-so-fine-you-so-fine-you-blow-my-mind' kind of look!"

Delia ignored them all and headed out to the floor to jump again. She noticed that the two fifth graders who had been fighting a few minutes before were giggling together, getting ready to jump again as well.

"Well, are you guys gonna turn for me or what?" she asked Misty and Charlene. They laughed and ran to pick up the ropes. Yolanda stayed on the sidelines, fixing her hair.

Delia jumped in from the left and went through the mandatory routine almost without thinking. Her mind was on Randy.

"Lookin' better, Delia!" Bomani shouted with encouragement. Delia never ceased to be amazed at how Bomani could see everything that was going on in six different areas of the gym. "Pick up those feet, Shantelle! Watch the ropes, DeLisa! Say, Shasta! Left foot, remember? Left foot!"

Bomani let them leave a little early because the gym was so stuffy and warm. Delia was glad to see her mother waiting for her in the parking lot. The air conditioner was cold and refreshing when she slid into the seat. "You need a ride, Randy?" Delia asked as she rolled down the window. "You better decide quick, because all the hot air is trying to sneak into the car!"

"You don't mind, Mrs. Douglas?" Randy asked, leaning his large frame down so he could peek into the window. "It sure beats taking the bus!"

"Of course not, Randy. Actually, it was my idea," Delia's mother told him. "Hop in."

Randy climbed gratefully into the back seat, inhaling deeply the cooled air. "Why do you think it's so hot, Mrs. D.?" he asked as they headed down the street.

"I read in the newspaper this morning that the weather is expected to be unusually hot like this until the end of the week," she told him. "My grandfather used to call this tornado weather," she added. "It's that time of year around here, you know."

"Makes me want to skip spring and jump right into summer vacation," Delia commented. "It's too hot for school." Delia usually glanced at the copy of the *Cincinnati Post* on the kitchen table when she got home from school, but except for the photos, the newspaper, along with the detailed weather forecast, was just a lot of gray fuzz.

"Hot for the next couple of days, at least, I heard. Then a cold front is supposed to come through." Delia's mother turned the air-conditioning fan up as high as it would go.

"We could use a couple of feet of snow!" joked Delia.

"Be for real. Maybe rain—humid and sticky, for sure," said Randy.

"You'll survive," Mrs. Douglas said calmly.

"Maybe not," Delia muttered under her breath. Mrs. Douglas didn't hear her, but Delia noticed that Randy did. Delia turned the radio on to her favorite station.

"So, is the team ready for the finals?" Mrs. Douglas asked, turning the music down.

"Oh, yeah, we're gonna kick butt!" Randy said with feeling. "Uh, excuse me, Mrs. D. We're going to do real good."

Mrs. Douglas laughed. "It's wonderful that the league has chosen Cincinnati to be the location of the world championships."

"Yeah, I guess it's cool for kids from Atlanta, who get to come here on a plane, but for us, we don't even get to go out of town! That sucks," Delia complained. "Last year we got to go to New York, and the year before that we went to Myrtle Beach. It's boring staying here at home."

"You still get to stay in a hotel and swim in the pool and do all the stuff you would have done out of town. Enjoy it and quit complaining," Mrs. Douglas said mildly.

"Being the hometown team gives us more power," Randy said.

"And more pressure for the jumpers," Delia added.

"But you get your picture in the paper and you get to be interviewed on TV. I heard Bomani talking to Clifton Grayson, the reporter, last week," her mother added wisely.

"Wow!" Delia said. "I think he's cute! I don't know if I'd be able to talk to him—I'd be so nervous."

"You probably won't have to say much—just jump like no tomorrow!" her mother told her. "Here's your place, Randy. You need anything, dear?" Mrs. Douglas asked.

"No thanks, I'm cool. Actually, I'm really hot, but you know what I mean," Randy said, laughing. "Thanks for the ride." Delia watched Randy glance at the windows of his apartment. They were dark.

Randy glanced back at Delia, gave her a smile, and headed into the building.

thirteen

IT WAS UNBEARABLY HOT IN THE HALLWAY, AND RANDY'S apartment seemed to pulse with heat. The cat greeted him at the door with a loud meow. He gave her some water in a dish, which she lapped up thirstily.

"Sorry about that, Cat," Randy said softly. He took a cool shower and made himself a large pitcher of Kool-Aid. It was so hot, he didn't even have an appetite.

He turned on a small fan in the living room, sat directly in front of it, took a deep breath, and dialed Delia's number. She answered on the first ring. "What's up?" he asked casually.

"Not much. It's too hot to think—too hot to breathe."

"Yeah, I feel ya. My cat is sitting here in front of my fan, sucking up all my cool air!" Randy laughed, but it sounded weak and hollow.

"Are you okay, Randy?" Delia asked. "What's going on?"

Randy sighed again. "Delia, I guess I gotta tell somebody." He stopped, pausing to think.

"What's wrong? You know you can trust me," Delia urged him.

"It's my dad."

"Did something happen on the road?"

"Uh, no, he, uh . . . he wants me to move to California

with him," Randy said suddenly. For some reason, he just could not bring himself to tell Delia the truth. "He called last night and wants me to meet him there next week."

"Next week!" Delia said, alarm in her voice. "Why can't he wait until the end of the school year? It's only a couple of months," she offered, her voice sounding strained.

"I told him I had to wait until after the Double Dutch tournament, then I guess I'm outta here."

"That's this weekend!" Delia repeated shrilly.

"I know," Randy answered quietly. He figured that if his dad had not returned by then, he would have to call the police and he'd be taken out of school, anyway. He wanted just a little more time. Time to be there for the tournament. Time to hope. Time to pray. "Delia?" Randy asked slowly.

"What, Randy?" Delia answered quietly.

"Dad said he would send me some money to get to California, but until he does, do you think . . . is there any way . . . I mean, I really hate to ask, but—"

"You need some money, Randy?"

"Naw, I'm okay. I was just teasing." Randy was suddenly embarrassed and sorry he had brought up the subject. But the woman from the electric company called every day, asking for more money, and the man from the rental company had simply laughed at the hundred dollars. Juggling it all made his head swim.

"I got fifty dollars for my birthday last month—Daddy always gives me money because he feels guilty that he's not with me like he used to be," Delia insisted. "I get to do with it what I want, and I'm bringing it to school tomorrow! I trust you, Randy, and I trust your dad. I know he's good for it!"

"Thanks, Delia. You don't know how much I appreciate it. I'll pay you back as soon as I hear from my dad—I promise." Even as he spoke, Randy worried about how he would ever be able to repay Delia if his father never came back.

"Don't worry about it, Randy."

"You got everything for our presentation tomorrow?" he asked, changing the subject. "You know my cat is gonna be the star of the whole show!"

Delia chuckled. "Yep, the tape is ready. Jesse's got one poster, Yolanda has the other, and you're bringing stuff to give the class—those little Martian pictures you drew, right? And you're right, bringing the cat was a cool idea."

"Well, me and my cat is tight." Randy laughed again. Delia made him feel relaxed and almost normal. "Yeah, I got the other handouts—the question sheets and stuff."

"It's gonna be a dynamite presentation, Randy. And then we get to see what the Tollivers came up with. Scary. Hey, my mom is calling me. I gotta go. I'll see you tomorrow."

"Peace, Delia. And thanks."

Randy got ready for bed, refusing to glance at the silent telephone. He slept restlessly, dreaming of his father. He woke up hot, sweaty, and hungry. He made himself a peanut butter and jelly sandwich and washed it down with the rest of the Kool-Aid. He chopped up the last hot dog into little pieces and gave it to the cat, who sniffed it like it was poison. "You get hungry enough, Cat, trust me, you'll eat it," Randy said as he got dressed for school. He grabbed all the materials for their presentation, stuffed them into his book bag, and headed out the door. The day was unbelievably hot already.

The weather was just weird, he thought. It just didn't feel right. The air even smelled funny.

By the time he got to school, he was already sweaty and uncomfortable. The heat inside the school, which was not air-conditioned, was thick and heavy. Kids moved in slow motion, fanning themselves during class, falling asleep in spite of themselves. Outside, although the air was unbearably oppressive and hard to breathe, the sky was not bright with sunshine. Instead it was a mustard yellow color, with odd, dusty-looking clouds hovering in it.

By third bell, time for English class, Randy just wanted to get out of there. The thought of jumping into an ice-cold swimming pool kept running through his mind as the sweat trickled down his back. Miss Benson, dressed in a sleeveless blouse and slacks, looked at her lethargic class as the bell rang. She took attendance and reminded the class that the state tests would begin next week. The class groaned and drooped even more.

"I hope Group Two has a dynamite presentation. We need something to wake us up. You guys ready? And Mr. and Mr. Tolliver? Are you two ready as well?"

Titan looked up. Dressed in black as usual, he didn't even look hot and uncomfortable like the others in the class. "We're ready," he said quietly.

Miss Benson smiled and said, "Good." She then looked to Delia's group and gave them a signal to begin.

Jesse, Yolanda, Delia, and Randy trooped to the front of the room and put their tape into the machine. Randy grinned. "Just wait!" he told the class. "We'll wake you up!" Loud rock music played for a few seconds, then Yolanda appeared on the screen. She was dressed in all red—red jeans, red shoes, red tank top—and her hair, instead of being pulled back into her usual ponytail, was down around her face. She looked directly into the camera and screamed.

Yolanda: EEEEEEEEEEEEEE!! They're coming! They're coming!

Delia: Who's coming? Quit that screaming!

Yolanda: The Martians. They landed on the roof of the school!

Delia: How do you know?

Yolanda: Randy told me.

Jesse: And you believe him?

Yolanda: He never lies.

Delia: But you do.

Jesse: Randy, how do you know there are Martians on the roof?

Randy: I heard them. I could hear their little slimy footsteps. They're coming this way!

Yolanda: See? I'm not lying this time. The Martians are coming to attack us. They're going to take us all back to

Mars and cut us into little pieces. We're gonna be chopped Martian stew!

Delia: I'm too young to die!

Randy: Well, I'm too tough to be eaten. Where are the Martians? I'm gonna go smash a couple of those little green suckers in their beady little heads.

Jesse: I'm with you, man. Let's head for the roof.

Yolanda: You can't! They have guns!

Delia: How do you know?

Yolanda: They always have guns! I've seen them in movies.

Jesse: She's right. We need weapons.

Delia: We're all gonna die!

Jesse: Well, I'm gonna die trying to fight for my freedom.

Randy: Yeah, what kills a Martian?

Delia: I don't know. What kills a person?

Jesse: Guns. Maybe we need Martian space guns.

Yolanda: What was that noise?

Delia: They're coming!

Randy: We're under attack!

Jesse: It's no use! We're gonna die!

Yolanda: EEEEEEEEEE!

Delia: Quit screaming.

Yolanda: If I'm going to die, I want to be noticed as I do it!

Jesse: The door is opening!

Randy: Here they come!

Delia: Good-bye, world!

On the screen the door opened slowly and the camera moved to the floor, where Randy's cat walked nonchalantly through the door. She yawned, curled up in a ball, and promptly went to sleep. Randy held a THE END sign in front of the camera, and the screen went black.

The class cheered and clapped as Randy, Delia, Jesse, and Yolanda took their bows. Miss Benson smiled with approval.

"Any questions?" asked Yolanda.

"Yeah, where did you get that dynamite red outfit?" a girl named Veronica asked from the back of the room. Everyone laughed again.

"You're supposed to ask questions about the project, Veronica," Randy complained.

"What were you trying to show?" asked Leeza. She looked at Miss Benson to make sure the teacher had noticed that she had asked a sensible question. Miss Benson nodded to let her know that she had.

"Sometimes people get scared of things that aren't even real," Randy answered.

"And they get all bent out of shape over things that aren't true," Delia added. "Sometimes it's more scary to believe the lie."

"And the truth is so simple that it's silly," said Randy.

"Of course, it could be that cats really ARE Martians in disguise, and we've been under attack for years," Yolanda joked.

Miss Benson thanked them, and the class clapped once more as the group sat down.

Another easy A, Delia thought to herself. *Ka-ching!*

"Can I go to the bathroom, Miss Benson?" Yolanda asked. "I promise I'll be quick, but I really, really have to go!"

"You sure you don't need open-heart surgery?" Miss Benson teased.

"That was last week. Today I think I have bursitis, or maybe meningitis. Whatever it is, it makes the patient have to go to the bathroom. I just gotta go. Please?"

"Okay, but hurry. You don't want to miss the next presentation, I'm sure."

"You got that right!" Yolanda grinned and hurried out of the room with the hall pass.

Miss Benson glanced at the clock, saw that there was plenty of time left in the class period, and glanced back at the Tolliver twins. "Okay, gentlemen," she said quietly. "You're on!"

fourteen

TITAN AND TABU ROSE TOGETHER FROM THEIR SEATS AT the same instant. They walked slowly to the front of the room, their boots stomping noisily and in unison on the scuffed classroom floor. The room was absolutely silent. Outside, the sky had darkened, and stone gray clouds began to accumulate. The leaves on the trees fluttered as though nervous in the unexpected winds, turning their backs to the sky. A cool breeze whipped through the open classroom windows with sudden fierceness as thunder rumbled in the distance. Miss Benson walked over to the windows and shut them quickly, making the classroom feel dismal and frightening, the electric lights a weak glow against the coming storm. Titan and Tabu stood in absolute silence at the front of the classroom. It was as if they had commanded the weather to be ominous as a natural background to their presentation.

Titan spoke first. "This book, *Lord of the Flies,* is about death—the death of children!" A huge flash of lightning, followed by a room-shaking blast of thunder, punctuated his statement. Delia jumped and gasped. The rest of the class looked around with fear. Miss Benson looked nervously out the window and at the two boys in the front. It seemed as if she had lost control, both inside and outside the classroom.

Tabu followed. "It's also about evil, and how much evil humans, even little boy humans, are capable of. In the book, Jack and his hunters go crazy and let evil take over their good sense. I think the author was tryin' to use kids to show that everybody has a little bit of evil in them. Everybody," he repeated with emphasis.

Titan continued, "And it's about fear—fear of what you don't know and don't understand." The lightning and thunder continued to build, and outside, the sky was almost as dark as night. Strangely, no rain had begun to fall. Just the thunder and the lightning and the thick, dark silences between each blast.

Tabu looked out the window. "If I told you that this was the end of the world, would you believe me?" he asked the class.

No one answered. Everyone was too scared.

Titan asked them, "And if I told you that me and my brother were mass murderers, would you believe that?" Another peal of thunder answered.

"Everybody at this school has acted just like the kids in this book," Tabu said fiercely. "You have treated us like monsters and killers, when we have done nothing but mind our own business. Maybe the evil is in you and not in us. Ever think of that?"

"Put it this way," Titan added. "Imagine a big, black rottweiler dog—maybe two of 'em. They look scary. They growl and bark a lot. You think they're mean or evil. But maybe it's you that's bad, not the dogs. Ever think about that?" Except for the rumbling of the thunder, the classroom was silent.

"But what about what you said on the TV show?" Delia

asked finally, blurting out the question before she had a chance to think. She shrank in her seat as another loud explosion of the strange, dry thunder shook the glass in the window frames.

The twins never had a chance to answer, for at that moment the wind rose with sudden fury, and the glass in one of the windowpanes shattered, shooting shards of glass like bullets across the room. Suddenly the lights flickered and went out, and darkness like nighttime enveloped the screaming students in the class. No one even noticed, except for Delia, when Tabu and Titan darted out of the classroom and into the hall.

An outside siren started to blow, low and ominous, as the inside siren of the school alarmed as well. Mr. Lazarro's voice came through the loudspeaker: "This is an emergency. This is NOT a drill. We have tornadoes in the area. Repeat. This is NOT a drill. Teachers, take your classes quickly and safely to designated areas. If you feel you cannot get to that area safely, ask students to lie face down, next to an inner wall, and away from the windows. I repeat! Tornadoes have been spotted in our area. This is a real emergen–" A crashing sound could be heard through the speaker, then all was silent. The sirens outside and the sirens inside wailed continuously.

Everyone screamed and ran from their seats, heading for the door. Miss Benson, although she was trembling, gathered all her strength and roared, "SILENCE!" The class, stunned for a moment, stopped and looked at her. "Lie on the floor, close to the wall–your bodies close together. No, away from the windows! You will be safe at that far wall. Huddle close to one another. Quickly!"

A gradual roaring, like a freight train thundering out of the sky, grew louder until it seemed to fill the room. The deafening noise was accompanied by the sound of breaking glass and thudding blocks of concrete.

Delia didn't have to be told twice. She rolled to the hard floor and was amazed at how cool it felt. Leeza huddled close to her, sobbing loudly. Delia couldn't see where Jesse and Randy were, and Yolanda, Delia remembered, was somewhere between the classroom and the bathroom. But soon she could think of nothing but the deafening noise and the sound of breaking and grinding. It was as if the school were being attacked by bombs. It shuddered and shifted from the onslaught. She covered her head and trembled with each jolt, with each crunching of glass, with each ripping of walls and bricks.

Suddenly, all was silent. The throbbing train blew into dust, and it was over. Outside, dark, ominous clouds hovered close to the horizon, as if they were not yet ready to leave such a scene. Slowly the students sat up and looked around. The classroom was a mess. Every window was cracked or broken. The TV on which they had just watched their silly video had crashed to the floor, glass and pieces of electronic parts all over the floor. Several student desks were broken.

Miss Benson stood hesitantly and checked on the students. "Jackie? Kamila? Omar? Zelda? Irene? Duffy? Princess? Andre? DaShawn? Zahir? Leeza?" Each student answered shakily that he or she was okay. Leeza was still crying, as were several other kids. Miss Benson continued checking for all her students, touching one and soothing the other. "Jesse? Randy? Veronica? Ishiko? Max? Delia?

Ching Lee? Bernardo? Hannah? Kristen? LaDonna? Shemika? Trevor? Yolanda?" Her voice grew suddenly high-pitched and frantic as she yelled to the huddled children on the floor, "Where's Yolanda?"

"Miss Benson!" Delia screamed. "Yolanda went to the bathroom! She didn't come back!"

"Oh, my goodness! Yolanda is out there somewhere!" Miss Benson said with fear in her voice. She picked her way across the debris in the room and walked slowly to the door, close to where Delia was sitting on the floor. Miss Benson carefully opened the door, checking to see if anything threatened to fall on her head. Delia peeked out with her. She could not believe her eyes. Pipes lay on the floor, and huge chunks of ceiling lay strewn about, tossed between broken glass and dangling wires. There was no sign of Yolanda or any other student. All was eerily still and dark. Miss Benson quietly closed the door.

"What are you doing?" screamed Delia. "We gotta find Yo Yo!"

Miss Benson put her hand on Delia's shoulder as she spoke to the class. "It's pretty bad out there, friends," she said solemnly. "It looks like we got hit by a tornado."

Delia felt dazed. It had all happened so fast. One minute they were sitting there, being scared by the Tollivers' presentation; the next minute, everyone was on the floor, huddling in terror as all the horses of heaven stomped through the room. Delia jumped as someone touched her back. She looked around and saw it was Randy.

"I've been right here the whole time," he told her. "I told you I got your back. It's gonna be okay." Delia started to cry. She was so scared and shaky, she didn't

116

know what else to do. "What about Yo Yo?" Delia wailed after a moment. "We gotta find her!" She headed for the door once more.

"Sit down, Delia!" Miss Benson commanded, blocking Delia's way to the door. "We don't know what kind of damage the building has sustained, and as long as I know that you are safe here, I'm going to do my best to keep you that way. This is a school, and all kinds of rescue people will be here in a matter of minutes to get you out safely. Yolanda is probably safer in the hall, anyway—that was where we were supposed to go in a tornado, remember? There just wasn't enough time. Now, we're staying put until help arrives. Got that?"

Delia sat down grudgingly. She tried not to think about what might have happened to Yolanda.

They could hear the sirens in the distance then—hundreds of them, it seemed. Help was on the way. *Hurry!* Delia prayed silently. *Please hurry!*

"Miss Benson, what will happen now?" Leeza asked shakily.

"I'm not sure, Leeza. If the rest of the building is as bad as our classroom, we're looking at some time off, it seems," she answered. "But I don't want to hear any cheering. People may have been seriously injured. Let's take one step at a time. I'm just glad that most of you are safe and accounted for."

"Miss Benson?" Delia said quietly.

"Are you okay, Delia?" Miss Benson asked kindly.

"I'm terrified about Yo Yo, but I'm fine. But Miss Benson, not everybody is accounted for. We forgot about Tabu and Titan. They ran out of the room when the storm first hit. They're not here."

fifteen

"OH, MY STARS! HOW COULD I HAVE FORGOTTEN ABOUT them?" Miss Benson glanced around the room with a look of disbelief and dismay—the twins were missing, and she had not noticed.

"I saw them run out, Miss Benson," Delia told her. "They heard the crashing and the roaring and they just jetted!"

"I pray that they are safe," Miss Benson said seriously. "I feel so responsible!" She sighed, sat on the floor with her students, and let her head drop into her arms. "We're just going to sit here quietly and wait," she told the class finally. "Help will be here soon."

"My grandfather lost his house when the tornado hit Cincinnati in the spring of ninety-nine," Leeza said to no one in particular.

"My uncle's store got demolished that year," added Veronica. "But the store right next to his only had a broken window."

"Tornadoes can be very capricious," Miss Benson explained. "I remember lots of tornadoes coming through here over the years—even when I was a kid. Some houses would be destroyed, while others were untouched."

"I hope my house is okay," whimpered Kristen. Everyone grew quiet. Delia figured everybody was thinking the same thing.

Gradually the dark sky beyond the broken windows started to brighten. Outside, Delia could hear the sounds of sirens, helicopters, and muffled megaphone voices shouting. At least a half hour passed, Delia figured—maybe longer. Students sat closely together whispering softly, afraid to move too much, afraid of broken glass or loose ceiling tiles.

Delia kept watching the door, hoping to see it open and Yolanda come bounding through with a smile and a tall tale.

Finally she heard voices and footsteps, and the sound of large objects scraping together in the hall outside the door.

"Anybody in there?" a muffled voice called out.

"Yeah! There's a bunch of us in here," Delia yelled, swinging open the door to face a fireman dressed in rescue gear, the most beautiful sight she had ever seen.

"Anybody hurt?" the fireman asked. "Your teacher here?"

"Yes, everybody here is fine—no injuries, thank goodness. But three students are not accounted for," Miss Benson reported. "Yolanda Pepper went to the bathroom just before the storm hit, and Tabu and Titan Tolliver—twins—ran out of the room, for what reason I do not know. How bad is the rest of the building?"

"The damage is pretty serious. It's going to take awhile to make sure everybody is out safely and we have an accurate assessment," the fireman replied.

"What about the rest of the city?" Delia asked. "Everybody here is scared."

"Most of the damage is in the few blocks right around

the school, although there are trees down all over the city. It looks like the school took a direct hit. The first weather reports are saying that twin twisters hit the school today. That's why there's so much damage," the fireman said.

"Twin tornadoes?" Delia whispered in quiet amazement. "Freaky."

"Let's see if we can get all of you out of here," the fireman said cheerfully. "I want you to form a human chain," he told the class. "Each one hold the wrist of the next one, and we'll march out of the building together. We've cleared a path for you through the rubble."

Randy grabbed Delia's wrist, and they headed out with the others. The scene in the hall was almost impossible to believe. They stepped carefully through what just hours before had been scuffed hallways but now looked like a bomb scene. The light fixtures in the ceiling were now shattered glass on the floor. What had been plaster walls, painted with what Delia called "that ugly schoolhouse green," now lay in huge chunks on the floor, decorated with wires, pipes, and dirt. The lockers—in this hall, at least—Delia noticed with a grim smile, stood like tall sentinels, undamaged and unmoved.

Several other chains of students were making their way through the hall, led by firemen who carefully escorted them out of the building. Delia searched every line for Yolanda, but didn't seen her among the crying, shaken kids. She did not see Titan or Tabu, either.

Delia could see, a few feet ahead of them, the front entrance of the school, where the metal detectors had stood this morning. It was now a gaping hole. The students walked in their chain, led by the fireman, through the hole and into what had become a bright and sunny day. The sky showed very little sign of the anger that had exploded from it so recently. The fireman led them to a spot on the grass across the street from the school.

"Wait here until the paramedic team can come check everyone out," he said to Miss Benson. "Keep them all together so we can account for each child and connect these kids with their parents. You got it under control?"

"I got it," Miss Benson said, but her voice showed strain.

Delia blinked and looked around her. She could scarcely believe her eyes. There was a huge piece missing from the roof of the school. Most of the windows were broken or gone. The front door had vanished. Ambulances, fire engines, police cars, and now, she noticed, news-camera trucks filled the small street where the school stood. A few kids had cell phones and were calling their parents. Hundreds of people ran about—students looking for siblings, teachers and administrators, and police officers trying to establish some sort of order.

Delia and Randy watched Mr. Lazarro, his hair covered with plaster dust, megaphone in his hand, run all over the area, comforting sobbing students, directing volunteers to aid stations, and reassuring parents who had started to arrive, fearful and frantic. It was chaos. And nowhere in that confusion could they see Yolanda.

"Do you think she's okay, Randy?" Delia asked. Even though they were sitting very close together, Delia felt cold and clammy. "I'm too scared to move, but I feel like I oughta be over there looking for her."

"She's gonna be fine," Randy assured her. "She's probably sitting up in one of those fire trucks, using the rearview mirror to comb her hair!"

Delia giggled a little, but she found she was trembling. "Do you think anybody got—you know—killed?" she asked Randy.

"Well, it looks pretty bad, but I don't see any smoke or flames. I guess that's a good sign. Looks like the roof took the biggest hit, from what we can see here, and I don't think there're any classrooms directly under that part—just the library. So there's a good chance that everybody got out safe. Even Yolanda," he added to soothe her.

At that moment a policewoman with a computer printout stopped by the area where the class huddled together around Miss Benson. "Any injuries?" the policewoman asked in an official tone.

"Fortunately, none," Miss Benson reported quietly.

"Any missing students?" the policewoman continued without looking up from her clipboard.

"Three. Yolanda Pepper. Tabu Tolliver. Titan Tolliver," Miss Benson reported as she continued to scan the crowd for her missing students.

"Is this your class list?" the officer asked Miss Benson as she pulled a sheet from her clipboard.

"Yes, this . . . uh . . . this was . . . third-bell English," Miss Benson said, stumbling over her words as she glanced at the sheet.

"The names of the students that are highlighted in green have parents waiting for them at the designated pickup area. Please release them to my assistant here, Officer Rodriguez. I will return for more students as we are able to identify parents who are waiting. It's a long process—please be patient."

Miss Benson called the names of about half the students, who gleefully went with the officer to be reunited with their parents. When Leeza's name was announced, she shouted, "Hallelujah!" Randy's and Delia's names were not called.

Jesse gave them both a high five as he left to find his mom. "Tell Yo Yo that this is what happens when you try to flush those school toilets!" Randy and Delia and even Miss Benson laughed as he left, picking his way through the confusion of fire hoses and wires and throngs of frantic people.

Mr. Lazarro stopped by their group to check on them for a moment. He looked worn and frazzled. "Cincinnati's had a lot of tornadoes over the years, but this is the first twister that's ever hit a school during school hours," he commented to Miss Benson as he gave the students candy bars that had been donated by the drugstore down the street.

"I guess we've been lucky," she said quietly.

"We need luck as well as blessings today," he replied emphatically. "I'm really worried about your three missing children." A firefighter called to him, and he hurried away.

Over the next hour, more students were located and reunited with parents, the crowds diminished, and the frenzy lessened a bit. At the next sweep by the policewoman, all but six of Miss Benson's students were taken to join their families. Yolanda seemed to have disappeared with the wind.

"Where're your folks, Delia?" Randy asked.

"My mom had a meeting in Columbus this morning.

It's about a two-hour drive, so I figure she's breaking all the speed records about now, trying to get home to me," Delia said, chuckling. "But when I called her on Leeza's cell phone I let her know I'm okay. Dad and Jillian are in San Francisco for the week, so it will be a while before they figure everything out. I'll call him when I get home. I know my mom will find me eventually—I'm not worried. Actually, I'm kinda glad. I want to be here when Yolanda shows up."

"I bet she has a REALLY big tale to tell!" Randy said with a smile that tried to hide his concern.

"What about your dad, Randy?" Delia asked. "Is he still in California? Oh, yeah, I almost forgot." She dug into her pocket of her jeans. "Here's the money I promised you could borrow." She stuffed a balled-up wad of money into his hand.

"I changed my mind. I don't need it—I'll be fine." He tried to give it back to her.

Delia insisted. "Now, shut up and take this! I know where you live. I'm not worried about getting it back."

Just as Randy was about to try to refuse once more, a huge, towering figure of a man loomed directly in front of them. "Hey!" his voice bellowed. "Are you two all right? I've been worried sick ever since I heard about the storm on the news. I had to check on my Queen Bees, and I guess that makes you the king or prince, or something, Randy." It was Bomani, who gave them both a big, comforting hug.

"Man, we sure are glad to see you!" Randy said with sincerity. "This has been one scary day! Miss Benson, this is Bomani, our Double Dutch coach and a real good friend." Miss Benson shook his hand and smiled.

"Where's Yolanda?" Bomani asked Delia. "Did she already find her mom and go home?"

Delia looked at Randy. "We don't know, Bomani," she said, trying not to cry. "Yo Yo went to the bathroom just before the storm hit, and she never came back. She hasn't come out of the building yet. As far as we know, she's still in there, but they're still bringing out kids a few at a time."

Bomani turned and looked at the severely damaged school and inhaled deeply. "Oh, my!" he whispered. "Oh, my."

Miss Benson said, "Several students are still unaccounted for. I have two other students who are missing as well. I'm sure the searchers will find them all. They simply must!" There was desperation in her voice.

"Has anyone that you know of been seriously injured, Miss Benson?" Bomani asked.

"No, thank God. So far, only cuts and scrapes. The last time the police officer stopped to give us an update, she said that they were amazed at how few serious injuries there were. It's as if the tornado whirled in carefully, destroying the building but missing the students."

"I sure hope Miss Yo Yo had her guardian angel with her in the bathroom," Bomani mused. He turned to Randy. "Your dad in town this week?" he asked abruptly.

Randy hesitated a moment. "Uh, he's gone for a few days, but I'll be fine. I'll go home after Delia's mom gets here."

"You'll do no such thing!" Bomani roared. "When Delia's mother gets here, you're coming home with me until we can get in touch with your father."

"I don't want to be a bother," Randy said. "You've got enough to handle with ten kids in the house."

"Can you wash dishes and small faces?" Bomani asked him. Delia smiled at the thought.

"Sure," Randy replied.

"Then you won't be a bother—you'll be a help."

"Well, okay, thanks, Bomani," Randy said gratefully. "Hey, what about my cat?"

"We can stop by your place and she can come with us," Bomani offered.

"No, man, my cat would have a heart attack with all those kids! If we could just stop by so I could feed her, that'd be cool."

"No problem," Bomani said, turning his attention to the policewoman who was walking toward the little group.

"Miss Benson?" the policewoman said in her usual formal tone.

"Yes, have you found them?"

"No, ma'am. We have called for search dogs to assist us. We have done a sweep through most of the building, and, as far as we can tell, only those three students are unaccounted for. But there's extensive damage inside. A couple of stairways have crumbled into piles of rock and rubble and are blocking our way. In addition, there are huge sections of walls that have collapsed, and we can't get past them yet. We've called for heavy equipment to help us clear these areas."

"Is the whole building destroyed inside?" Miss Benson asked.

"Amazingly," the fireman replied, "in some areas the windows are unbroken and the floors show nothing more than the scuffed footprints of the students who went to class this morning. In another area, the only problems were a water fountain that would not shut off and a clock that showed the incorrect time."

"Oh, that has nothing to do with the tornado," Randy quipped. "That's the fountain on the second floor—it's always broken!"

"And no two clocks in our building ever indicate the same time!" Delia added.

The fireman smiled and turned to Miss Benson. "The parents of the missing students are here. Would you like to speak to them?"

"Oh, yes! I feel like it's my fault!"

"It wasn't your fault, ma'am. The storm is the criminal here."

Mrs. Tolliver and Mrs. Pepper rounded the corner then, holding hands. Both women had been crying. Delia ran to Yolanda's mother and hugged her, letting the tears fall finally. "I'm so worried about Yo Yo!" Delia sobbed. "Where is she?" Mrs. Pepper could not answer, and let her tears join Delia's.

Mrs. Tolliver stood to one side, silently watching. Miss Benson approached her. "Mrs. Tolliver? I'm Miss Benson, your sons' English teacher. Your boys were giving an oral report in class—a very powerful presentation, I might add—when the storm hit and they simply ran out of the room in the midst of all the confusion of thunder and screaming and flickering lights."

"I wonder why they ran out of the room like they did," Delia muttered loud enough for Mrs. Tolliver to hear.

Mrs. Tolliver looked directly at Delia. "My boys are afraid of storms," she said clearly.

Randy, who was standing next to Miss Benson and Mrs. Tolliver, asked then, "Excuse me, but did you say that Tabu and Titan are scared of storms?"

127

Mrs. Tolliver replied, "Yes, but don't you ever tell them I said so. Their father got killed in a terrible thunderstorm when they were very young—a tree in our backyard fell just as he was running into the house. When I got home from work, I found the twins huddled together in the dark, their father lying dead in the mud in the backyard. They've been terrified during storms every since."

"So that explains a lot," Miss Benson mused. "I know you must be frantic with worry, Mrs. Tolliver," she added. "There's no telling what kinds of memories a storm like this can stir up. I'm glad you're here so you can reassure them that everything will be okay. Let's pray they'll be found soon."

"I know they're big, and I even know they try to be bullies, but they're still my babies," Mrs. Tolliver said quietly.

"But what about all the stuff they said on the talk show?" Delia asked timidly.

Mrs. Tolliver sighed. "My boys have never been happy children, but they're not bad kids," she began.

"They've never actually done anything wrong, as far as I know," Miss Benson told her, "but they have managed to frighten quite a few people."

"They like putting on like they're mean, but they're really just two kids who are afraid of getting close to anybody. They use each other and depend on each other so much that they block out the rest of the world—even me." Delia couldn't believe how sad she looked.

"They've managed to do a pretty good job of intimidating their classmates, too," Miss Benson said.

"I'm sorry," Mrs. Tolliver said. "That television show was a mistake." She sighed again. "Money has been very tight lately. I'm only working part-time," Mrs. Tolliver continued, "and I'm NOT going on welfare. I have no idea where they got my name, but the producers of the show called me and offered me more money than I could make in six months if me and the boys would appear on the program. I couldn't turn it down. I'm sorry if they frightened everybody. It was mostly big words and empty threats. The producers loved it."

"I told you those TV shows are fake!" Randy whispered to Delia.

A squawking noise interrupted the conversation. The policewoman spoke into the walkie-talkie on her shoulder and said briskly, "Yes, sir!" She turned to the group standing there on the grass. "You might want to come with me. Someone is emerging from the building."

Randy grabbed Delia's hand as they ran ahead of the adults toward the school. Long strips of yellow caution tape had been strung around large areas of the building, but they ducked under it as they saw three dusty figures emerge, not from the hole where the front door used to be, but from the side of the building. Tabu Tolliver, his black shirt torn, a huge, bleeding gash on his chest, staggered forward. Next to him stumbled his brother, Titan, his face dirty, his eyes blinking in the sunlight. In his arms he carried the unmoving figure of Yolanda Pepper, her ponytail dangling.

sixteen

DELIA THOUGHT HER HEART WOULD EXPLODE IN HER chest. *Oh, my God,* she whispered in prayer, *please don't let Yo Yo be dead. Please.* She couldn't move for a moment, but Mrs. Pepper screamed, "My baby!" and ran past Delia and Randy to her daughter. A paramedic got to the trio first and asked Titan to set Yolanda down on the ground. He did so more gently than Delia ever would have expected. Tabu looked dazed. Both boys seemed to be confused by the quickly growing crowd of paramedics, police, reporters, and students. Titan staggered a little, then sat down next to Yolanda, who still had not moved. The paramedic knelt over her. Another paramedic began to treat Tabu's wounds while the police tried to push back the crowd of onlookers.

Mrs. Pepper had to be restrained from knocking everyone aside to get to her daughter. "Let us take a look at her, ma'am," one of the paramedics said. "Give us just a few minutes, okay?"

Mrs. Tolliver quietly slipped around the crowd and sat on the grass close to her sons. She hugged each boy tightly and kissed each of them on the forehead. They looked embarrassed, but they didn't pull away from her. The gash on Tabu's chest was deep enough to require a few stitches, the paramedic told her as he cleaned the wound, and Titan mostly had just cuts and bruises.

Delia stood trembling, close to Mrs. Pepper, as they waited for word of Yolanda's condition. Yolanda looked pale and lifeless lying there on the damp grass, a medium-sized lump swelling on the left side of her forehead. The paramedic broke a small plastic vial and passed it under Yolanda's nose. Delia could smell it even from where she stood. Yolanda coughed and fluttered her eyelids, turning her head to get away from the smell of the ammonia.

In another moment, she had opened her eyes fully and looked around in bewilderment. Delia imagined what Yolanda must have seen looking up at the faces peering down at her, with clear blue sky above. "Am I dead?" Yolanda finally asked. The tension was broken. Everybody laughed with relief.

"No, baby," said her mother, who had finally pushed her way to her daughter's side, "but we thought you were. Do you remember what happened?"

Yolanda was silent for a moment. She looked confused. "I had to pee really bad, and I was almost to the bathroom. Then it's like the hall blew up, and I got scared and started running. Pieces of ceiling were falling, and I swear I heard a train coming down the hall. I got turned around and confused, and I fell. Then I looked up and I saw the Tollivers running full speed, like the train was chasing them or something. I was afraid they were chasing *me!* I heard another huge crashing noise, I felt something hit me on the head, and everything went dark. That's all I remember, until just now, when somebody who's wearing some really gross perfume got too close to my nose and I woke up here."

"You were in a tornado, Yolanda—all of us were," Delia told her. "The whole school is messed up. Nobody could find you when it was over, and we were really scared. And get this! The Tollivers weren't chasing you—they saved your life. Titan carried you out."

Yolanda turned her head toward Titan, wincing in pain. "For real?" she asked him.

Titan shrugged his shoulders. "No big deal," he said. Both of the boys looked uncomfortable with all the attention directed toward them.

"So how did you manage to save my baby girl?" Mrs. Pepper asked Titan. "You're a real hero, you know. Are you going to be okay? Is there anything I can do to help?"

"Mom, let him answer. You're talkin' as fast as those winds were blowing!" Yolanda interrupted.

Titan glanced at Yolanda with a look of thanks on his face. "We never planned to be no heroes. We heard the storm and we jetted, 'cause that classroom just didn't look safe," he began.

Tabu, wincing a bit as he touched the bandage on his chest, continued. "We saw Yolanda in the hall just before everything went ballistic. A big hunk of ceiling dropped down on us. I saw Titan fall down. Then another piece hit me, and I guess it knocked me out. The next thing I remember was him shakin' me."

Titan added, "We sat there in the dark for a long time, then we figured we'd better try to get out, so as we were moving pieces of wall and stuff, we saw Yolanda layin' there."

"We thought she was dead," Tabu said quietly.

"So I picked her up and brought her out. Like I said, no big deal." Titan looked embarrassed.

Yolanda insisted on sitting up, even though the pain made her wince. "Hey, I don't know about you, but I think I'm a VERY big deal!" She smiled at the twins. "You two are straight up. How can I ever thank you?"

Tabu let a shadow of a smile show through. "Win at Double Dutch this weekend," he said.

"How do you know so much about Double Dutch?" Delia asked, shocked.

They didn't answer, but walked with their mother, who led them to the waiting ambulance so they could be checked at the hospital for further injuries. The crowd cleared a path for them and, as they walked, a few people began to applaud. The clapping got louder and stronger and swelled to cheers as the boys climbed into the back of the ambulance and were driven away.

By this time, Yolanda was on a stretcher and also headed for an ambulance, even though it was pretty clear that she had no really serious injuries. She looked at her mother and Bomani, who walked beside her. Delia and Randy walked on the other side. "Will I still be able to jump this weekend?" Yolanda asked.

"Let's just make sure you're okay first. We will do what the doctors say," her mother replied.

"Is my hair a mess?" Yolanda asked Delia.

"Totally wiped out," Delia replied, laughing.

"I hope they have bathrooms at the hospital," Yolanda said as she was being lifted into the ambulance. "I never did get to pee!"

Just as the ambulances were leaving, Delia's mother arrived, running toward the small crowd that remained. She grabbed Delia and hugged her for a very long time. "Are you sure you're all right, sweetie?" her mother asked with tears in her eyes.

"I'm fine, Mom, really, and so is Yo Yo, I think. It was the strangest thing—she got rescued by the Tollivers! I'll tell you all about it in the car. Let's go home. Is our house okay? Oh, Mom. I was so scared! It was like some kind of monster was attacking—nothing seemed real. Even the sky was the wrong color. And then I thought for sure Yolanda was dead."

As they all walked together to the parking lot, Delia's mother touched Miss Benson's arm, who, finally sure that all her students were safe and accounted for, walked wearily with them. "I just want to thank you for keeping my daughter—and the rest of children, as well—safe today. You, too, were a hero."

"I didn't do anything special," Miss Benson said in genuine surprise. "I just sat with them until help arrived. I was as scared as they were."

"But they didn't know that," Mrs. Douglas told her. "They looked to you, and you were there—keeping them safe."

"Thanks, Mrs. Douglas," Miss Benson told her as they shook hands in the parking lot. "I really needed to hear that. It's been a rough day."

"Go home and get some rest," Delia's mom said gently. "You deserve it." She gave Miss Benson a hug, and the exhausted teacher finally got in her car and drove away.

"Did you hear anything else on the news, Mrs. Douglas?" asked Bomani, who was walking behind them with Randy.

"The last news report I heard just as I got here said that

the school will be closed for at least the next three weeks—probably until the end of the school year," she told them. "And the state proficiency tests scheduled for next week have been postponed—indefinitely."

Delia whooped with delight as she got into her mother's car. "Call me later!" she yelled to Randy.

seventeen

RANDY GRINNED AND WAVED TO DELIA, FEELING RELIEVED and frightened as well. He wondered how he should handle this. He was going to have to tell Bomani about his dad.

At Bomani's house his children huddled around Randy, making him tell the story of the storm over and over again. The ones old enough for school had practiced the usual tornado drill, but nothing more exciting than a little wind and thunder had occurred at their schools. To have somebody at their house who had lived through a direct hit from twin twisters made Randy a hero, and they peppered him with questions all evening.

The news reports on television told of the terrible damage to the building, the lack of serious injury to students or staff, and the heroism of Titan and Tabu Tolliver. The stations kept rerunning the film from their appearance on the talk show and speaking in very excited terms about this turn of events. Dozens of reporters were camped out on the lawn of the small Tolliver house, but they said no one inside would agree to come out and talk to them.

Randy ate a huge dinner, interrupted only by giggles and questions from Bomani's children. He thanked Bomani and his wife for allowing him to stay there for a day or two.

"Have you been able to reach your dad yet?" Bomani

asked as he and Randy washed the dishes while Bomani's wife put the kids to bed.

"Uh, no, not yet. His cell phone is turned off," Randy said honestly.

"When is the last time you talked to him? He must have heard about the storm—it's been on all the national news stations. Did you call home and check your answering machine to see if he's called you? I know he will be worried if he can't find you."

"There was no message," Randy said quietly. He clenched and unclenched his fists. He had finally had enough. The burden of a missing father was too much to carry along with the stress and the fear of the day. "Bomani? We're straight, right? You always tell us in Double Dutch that if we've got problems, we should tell you, right?"

"Of course," Bomani said, setting down the plate he was wiping. "What's wrong, Randy? You can tell me anything. I'm here for you. You know that."

Randy sighed. "I haven't seen or heard from my father in more than two months," he blurted out finally. "I think he's deserted me, just like my mom did," Randy added in a whisper.

"How have you been living all this time?" Bomani asked. He sat down with a thud on the sofa.

"By myself. Me and my cat. I just knew he'd be home any day, so I didn't tell anybody. I didn't want to call the police, because I was afraid they'd put me in some foster home or they'd get my dad in trouble for leaving me. So I just managed. He left me a little money, but that's all gone, and I'm at a place where I just don't know what to do." It felt so good to finally tell somebody.

Bomani was silent for a while. "You'll stay here for the time being," he said finally. "Then we'll start investigating what's going on. And don't worry—nobody is going to make you go to a foster home, and nobody is going to get your dad in trouble. I know he wouldn't desert you, Randy. He adores the ground you walk on. There has got to be an explanation, and we will find it—I promise."

Randy felt weak with relief. Bomani gave him a big hug and looked him straight in the eye. "I wish you had told me sooner. We're a family in Double Dutch. Families don't keep secrets like that—they help each other. Don't worry. We're going to figure this out. Now, here's a blanket. You get your choice—the big couch or the little one to sleep on."

Randy grinned. "The big one, of course. And thanks, Bomani. I feel like a hundred pounds have been lifted off my back."

"Good thing, 'cause I think you ate a hundred pounds of food tonight!"

"Bomani? Can I call Delia before I go to sleep?" Randy asked. "I want to see how Yolanda is doing."

"Sure, and let me know how they both are. Today was unbelievable. I'm so glad you are all safe."

"You think we'll still be able to have the tournament this weekend?" Randy asked as he tossed the blanket on Bomani's big, comfortable sofa.

"I know today has been traumatic, but as soon as we get ourselves together and start to breathe normally, we're going to have the finest World Championship Double Dutch Tournament the world has ever seen!" Bomani said with encouragement. "We're gonna be jumping with the best of them all day Friday and Saturday."

"I'm glad. I think we all need something to think about besides the tornado. I sure hope Yo Yo is okay."

"Me, too. And Randy? I'm going to make some inquiries on my own about your father, but if nothing has changed by Monday, we're calling the police. Bet?"

"Bet. Thanks again, Bomani—for everything."

"No problem. Give my best to Delia." Bomani headed up the stairs.

Randy dialed Delia's phone number, feeling better than he had in weeks. "Hey, Delia," he said when she picked up the phone. "Have you heard from Yolanda?"

"I just got off the phone with her. She's back home and she's gonna be okay. The doctor said she had a mild concussion, which is a big word for a bad bump on the head."

"Oh, goodness, now we're gonna have to listen to her stories of concussions and medical complications for months!"

Delia laughed. "It's already started. She told me that while she was unconscious she saw angels who lifted her up and carried her out."

"She didn't see angels—she saw the Tollivers, the last people that I would confuse with anything from heaven," Randy said.

"You got that right," agreed Delia. "But you know, maybe we *have* been unfair to them. Maybe they're not as bad as we've been making them out to be."

"Maybe," Randy said thoughtfully.

"It's not every day you save somebody's life—even if they didn't really plan to," Delia replied.

"Well, I'm sure glad they did. Yolanda's kinda far out there sometimes, but I'm so glad she's all right. I don't even care about her tall tales." Randy chuckled.

"Me neither. She said the doctor told her if she rests for the next few days, there's no reason why she can't jump in the tournament," Delia added.

"That's good news. She should have no problem resting with the school closed down. You know, when I was little, I used to dream about the school blowing up or burning down. I never really believed it would happen."

"I know. It makes me a little sad that the school is messed up, but I am so glad we don't have to take that state test!" Delia said with glee.

"You know they'll make us take it eventually," Randy reminded her.

"Yeah, but by then Double Dutch Championships will be over, and I won't have to deal with one before I get to do the other!" Delia reasoned.

"Whatever," Randy said. "You know, Bomani told me we've raised enough money for all of us to stay in the hotel downtown with the rest of the teams. We check in Thursday, he said."

"Super!" Delia replied. "That's the best part of a trip—eating pizza at midnight, swimming in the hotel pool, running from room to room, and—"

"And getting yelled at by Bomani and the chaperones when we do that!"

"I'm glad you're at Bomani's house, Randy, especially with your dad so far away."

"Me, too," Randy added with real honesty. "I'm gonna sleep good tonight on this big, fat, lumpy sofa."

"I gotta go now, Randy. My other line is beeping. Talk to you tomorrow."

"Later."

eighteen

As Randy hung up, Delia clicked over to the other line. It was Yolanda again.

"Guess what, girl?" Yolanda began.

"What's up? You okay?"

"Yeah, my head is feeling better already, and the swelling is going down a lot. But you'll never guess who I just talked to."

"Who?" Delia asked. "A reporter?"

"Yeah, two or three of them have called. I think I'll be in the paper tomorrow—with my hair a mess! But that's not what I'm talking about. I just got off the phone with the Tollivers!"

"No way!" Delia was blown away by this bit of information. "What did they say? Did you call them, or did they call you?"

"I called them. I figured I needed to thank them properly. And I felt bad because all of us have spent so much time being scared of them that we never even tried to tell them apart."

"You're right, Yo Yo. Tell me what you talked about."

"Well, Tabu was on the upstairs phone, and Titan was downstairs, and after I thanked them upside down and backward, I asked them to tell me more about how they found me. Tabu said they ran out of the classroom because they were scared and didn't want any of the kids to see them that way. Then things started falling from the ceiling, and they didn't know where to go. The walls kinda caved in on them, and they were probably both out cold for a while."

"So they weren't following you or chasing you like you thought?"

"No, they stumbled over me in the darkness after they got themselves together and tried to find their way out. Dumb luck, I guess."

"But what took so long?" Delia asked. "We waited for what seemed like hours—we thought you were dead, Yo Yo." Delia shuddered.

"I did, too, for a minute," Yolanda replied with a short laugh. "Titan said huge pieces of wall or ceiling or something had fallen all around them, and it took the two of them quite a while to move stuff out of the way so they could find their way out of the building."

"Why didn't they call for help?" Delia asked.

"They told me they figured they could get out by themselves, and they also didn't think many people would care that they were missing," Yolanda said.

"That's sad," Delia commented. "But what made them decide to rescue you?"

"I was there, so they just carried me out with them. 'No big deal,' Tabu told me."

"Awesome!" Delia whispered. "So what else did they say?"

"We talked about stuff they like and what music they listen to. They like all the same stuff we do—same music, same groups, same TV shows. It was amazing. Then I asked Tabu what he meant when he told me to win at Double Dutch."

"That blew me away when he told you that this afternoon," Delia said. "What did he say?"

"You're not gonna believe this!" Yolanda began.

"Is this another one of your lies, Yo Yo?" Delia asked, laughing.

"No, girl, this is for real. I couldn't make this up in a million years. Titan told me that he and Tabu both liked me, and they knew everything about me—my birthday, my favorite color, and how much I love Double Dutch. Can you believe that? He said they were at the city and the state tournaments—sitting in the bleachers, watching me jump."

"Freaky!" Delia said. "I saw them up there that one time, but who woulda thought they were watching *you!* What did you tell them?"

"What could I say? Men are just attracted to me!"

"Get outta here!"

"Hey, my mom is calling. She wants to baby me some more, and I'm gonna let her. I'll talk to you tomorrow," Yolanda said cheerfully.

"Okay, later. I can't wait to see tomorrow's newspaper! Our school, and you, and the not-so-terrible Tollivers are the talk of the town!" Delia hung up the phone. She knew she couldn't *read* tomorrow's paper, but the pictures would be wonderful.

nineteen

DELIA WAS TREMENDOUSLY HAPPY. SHE DIDN'T HAVE TO go to school. She didn't have to take the state proficiency test. And she didn't have to worry about reading at all. Between extra Double Dutch practices, getting their things ready for the hotel trip, and keeping up with all the news reports about the tornado and its damage, there was little time to reflect on the future beyond the coming weekend.

Yolanda recuperated quickly and was thrilled that her picture, along with the twins', not only made the front pages of the *Cincinnati Enquirer* and the *Cincinnati Post* newspapers, but would also be featured in *People* magazine as well.

Thursday night the team checked into the Westin Hotel, along with several other teams from around the country. "There're the kids from New York," whispered Yolanda. "Stan's Pepper Steppers—they're really good."

"Yeah, I remember," Delia answered. "South Carolina always has a really good team too. Isn't that them just getting out of that bus?"

"I hope that cute dude who can jump so fast comes this year. He is so fine!" Yolanda said with a grin.

"Don't you think you have enough trouble with twins in love with you?" Delia asked, laughing.

"Who said anything about love? I just like to be

admired!" Yolanda responded. "But the Tollivers did say they would come on Saturday to watch us."

"Good. You know, one of the teams last year had twin boys on its doubles team. They were dynamite. You think the Tollivers might want to try to jump Double Dutch with us?"

"Who knows?" Yolanda shrugged and looked up at Bomani, who handed her a room key. "Let's check out the room. I want to see what's on HBO."

"You've got HBO at home!" Randy teased as he tossed his bag onto his shoulder.

"It's different in a hotel room," Yolanda reasoned. "My mother isn't here to tell me to turn it off!"

Yolanda and Delia, carrying more than they would ever need for two days, pushed the elevator button for the seventh floor. Misty and Charlene shared the room next to them on one side, and Bomani and Randy were across the hall. The rest of the team and a few parents took most of the other rooms on that floor. The room was cool and perfect, the way their rooms at home would never be.

"This is the life!" Yolanda sighed as she bounced on the bed, the remote control in her hand.

"Hey, I've got a taste for some candy," Delia said after she unpacked her things. "I think I'm going down to the lobby to get some Twizzlers or a Twix. Want something?"

"Yeah, bring me a Hershey's bar. It's sweet and smooth and perfectly chocolate, just like me," Yolanda answered.

"That bump on your head must have been more serious than they thought," Delia teased. "You're trippin'." She took the key and walked down the long, carpeted hall to the elevator. In the lobby she looked around, saw the little shop where candy was sold, then noticed another bus of Double

Dutch teams unloading. She wandered outside to the loading area to see where this new group was from.

The Canadian team, Delia realized. She remembered them—they were good. Several of their teams took first place last year. *This was going to be the bomb,* she thought excitedly. *The Queen Bees are going to blow it up this year!* Delia watched them unload, waving at the girls she remembered from last year, knowing they would be strong competitors.

Delia looked up and down the busy street. She loved being downtown. It was so busy and full of life—it didn't even seem like the same city she lived in, she thought. She wandered out to the curb, gazing at the announcements for rock concerts, comedy clubs, and political candidates that had been tacked to the telephone pole there, wishing once again that the words would make sense to her. The pole was pocked and gouged with staples and nails and holes from old announcements that had been replaced by new ones. Near the bottom was a typed sheet of white paper with a picture on it that caught her attention. It almost looked like . . . but it couldn't be. Yes, it looked like Randy's father! Delia gasped. What was Randy's father doing on a poster?

She ripped the paper off the pole and gazed at the fuzzy photo in front of her. It was definitely Randy's father, unsmiling and looking a little confused, and a lot thinner than Delia remembered. *He looks like a criminal,* Delia thought, and was instantly ashamed for thinking it.

What did it say? Tears of angry frustration filled her eyes. She really *needed* to be able to read this. She could read some of the smaller words, but not enough to patch together a sentence to figure out what the flyer said.

So this is why Randy had acted so funny when she'd asked him about his father. And why he'd asked to borrow the money! His dad was in trouble. She wondered if he was running from the law, if he'd committed some terrible crime and was hiding from the police! *No wonder Randy has been stressed!*

Delia checked a couple of the other telephone poles, but she saw no other papers like the one she held in her trembling hand. For a moment, she considered throwing it away, but she didn't know what to do. Show Randy? But she felt he already knew his dad was in trouble—that's why he'd been acting so weird. If she told Bomani or her mother, they'd have to call the police. Taking deep breaths to calm her beating heart, she decided the best thing to do was to help Randy keep it a secret. Randy would be glad she was such a good friend, Delia thought shakily.

Satisfied with her decision, Delia folded the flyer several times and stuffed it into the pocket of her shorts. She headed back to the elevator, remembered the candy, bought several bars, and returned to the room.

"What took you so long?" Yolanda asked. "I'm up here about to die from lack of chocolate in my bloodstream. The doctors told me that chocolate is good for my concussion."

"Uh, long line," Delia said as she touched the folded paper in her pocket. "Oh, and the Canadian team is here. They're looking good."

"Not as good as us!" Yolanda said as she licked her candy bar.

"Why do you do that?" Delia asked, making a face of disgust.

"'Cause it freaks you out!" Yo Yo grinned. "Hey, Bomani called. He wants a team meeting in fifteen minutes. He said we get pizza afterward."

"Great! You're not gonna lick the pizza, too, are you?" Delia laughed.

"Now THAT's disgusting!" Yolanda replied.

At the team meeting Bomani discussed rules and gave them dozens of reminders. "Remember to keep your T-shirts tucked in at all times, ladies—fifteen-point deduction if you forget. And don't forget, if you enter the ropes from the right, you must exit on the left. In the compulsories, thirty seconds for singles, forty for doubles, and make sure those knees come up waist-high! Watch out for penalty points, and aim for bonus points." Finally, he said with fierce, passionate power in his voice, "Double Dutch is a TEAM sport, not an individual one. Each team is only as strong as the rope turners and the jumper or jumpers. Unless all parts of the team are working together like a machine, you will not be successful!"

Delia had heard it all many times, but she listened with interest and tried to remember every suggestion that Bomani made. She had learned from past tournaments that sometimes it was the attention to little details that made the difference between first and second place. She tried not to think of the WANTED poster hidden in her pocket as she watched Randy in a corner of the room, ironing their team shirts for tomorrow. She knew it was the part of his job he liked the least, but every shirt would be crisp and perfect by morning.

As Bomani passed out the pizza, he took the time to tell each girl how special he thought she was, how proud he was to have her on his team, and how proud he would be of her tomorrow, no matter how she scored. Delia and Yolanda smiled as broadly as the kids on the third-grade team because Bomani really meant what he said—Double Dutch made them all special.

"You sure you're okay to jump tomorrow, Yolanda?" Bomani asked for the fifteenth time as Yolanda and Delia were heading back to their room.

"Honest, Bomani, I'm okay. My mom took me to the doctor again yesterday and he said I was fine. You know my mother wouldn't even let me out of the house if she thought I was in any danger. I'm ready—just relax."

"Okay. Good. You two get some sleep now—breakfast is at seven. We have to be at the gym by eight-thirty for warm-ups," Bomani told them. Delia waved to Randy as they left the room.

She wondered again if she should tell him she knew about his dad. But she couldn't. She couldn't embarrass him like that. Could she tell Yolanda? No, that would be selling out a friend—telling his business to the world. She decided to wait until the tournament was over. Then maybe she could just let him know that if he needed anything, he could count on her. What she probably should do is throw the thing away—he'd never know. She walked slowly behind Yolanda, who never even noticed Delia's frown of confusion.

twenty

BY FRIDAY MORNING AT NINE THE GYM WAS FULL OF noisy, excited, jumping young people. T-shirts identified them from dozens of other states, as well as several foreign countries. Every shirt was tucked in; every tennis shoe was clean and tied tightly to prevent accidental slips or trips. Ropes flew in the halls, on the steps in front of the building, and in every possible clear space in the huge gym at the University of Cincinnati. The tapping of the young feet and the rapping of the twisted ropes on the floor built up a syncopated rhythm of excitement.

Friday's events would take almost all day, Delia knew. Every singles team—from third grade through the open divisions—had to be evaluated in compulsory, speed, and freestyle events. The whole procedure would be repeated for the doubles teams. With more than three hundred teams represented, it seemed it would take forever, but that evening, the top five teams in every grade and every division would be posted. Those would be the teams to compete in the finals on Saturday.

The judges, dressed in all white, stood near each team with counters and clipboards, making sure that every step was counted, every turn was registered, and every miss was deducted from the score. When the Queen Bees were called for singles, Delia and Yolanda and Charlene gave each other a high five, and marched to the center of the gym floor. Randy gave them a wink from where he watched with Bomani in the stands.

The buzzer sounded. Delia jumped the compulsory round to perfection. But Bomani always told them that by eighth grade the compulsories *ought* to be perfect. Charlene jumped the speed round while Yolanda and Delia turned. She missed once, but she didn't let it frazzle her concentration. She jumped right back in, head down, knees low, tapping incredibly fast to the whistling of the ropes. She jumped a dynamite 350 jumps in the thirty-second time period. The three of them were pleased.

For their freestyle routine they managed to include several complicated tricks—including a backward push-up and a one-hand flip—without missing or getting tangled in the ropes. Bomani and Randy gave them a thumbs-up sign as they walked off the floor feeling triumphant.

"You think we made the finals?" Yolanda asked Delia as they went to the lobby to get hot dogs.

"I think we did pretty good. Unless South Carolina or Georgia beats us out with their fancy freestyle stuff, I think we've got a good shot. We didn't make any major mistakes. Is your head okay? You feeling all right? You know we still gotta do doubles in a couple of hours."

"Yeah, I never felt better. Really."

"Good. Then let's go back in—I want to see what the Japanese team does in their freestyle routine. They're awesome. It's like they're dancing with the ropes. Are your parents coming tomorrow?" Delia asked.

"Yeah, they had to work today. My father told me we'd

better make the final five so he'd have something to see tomorrow. You know how he is."

"Don't sweat it. I think we'll be there. I have faith." Then Delia asked Yolanda slyly, "So, are both your boyfriends coming tomorrow? And what about Jesse?"

Yolanda laughed. "Jesse is in Cleveland with his dad—something about male bonding because of the almost-tragedy at school. And I don't know if the twins will show or not. One thing you can say about them: They sure aren't predictable!"

"What are you wearing to the DD party tonight?" Delia asked.

"A prom dress," Yolanda tossed back at her. "What about you?"

"Something cool—all that jumping in such a small area makes me sweaty."

"Well, in that case I'll wear a swim suit!" Yolanda laughed.

That evening at the party Delia took a moment to get a Coke, smiling to herself as she watched teams from all over the country jump together. Jackie and Shana were challenging some kids from Taiwan to speed jumps. Charlene and Misty were teaching some younger jumpers from California how to do some fancy rope tricks. Even Randy was jumping with some of the kids from Canada. Competition was forgotten for the moment; everyone was friends for the evening, sharing the one thing they all loved—the magic of the ropes.

The list of the final five in each grade and division was posted shortly after the party broke up. Fourteen of Cincinnati's eighteen teams were represented, including the third-grade singles team and doubles team, the fourth-grade doubles and freestyle teams, and at least one or two teams from each grade level. Delia's eighth-grade team was selected in all three divisions—singles, doubles, and free-style. Delia cheered and hugged Yolanda and Charlene and Misty. This was too good to be true.

The girls were elated, although the teams that did not place were initially disappointed. Bomani made sure no one felt sorry for herself and that every single girl encouraged the teams that would represent them all on Saturday.

The next morning, dressed in crisp white shorts and freshly ironed T-shirts, once again thanks to Randy, the Queen Bees marched proudly into the gym with the rest of the Ohio teams in the grand parade of states as the music of the Olympics piped through the speakers. Every single competitor, whether she or he had been selected for the finals or not, marched with pride and dignity. Parents took pictures and videotapes; reporters from local TV stations, as well as CNN, hovered close by; and the tension was thick enough to slice. Delia's mom sat with Yolanda's parents on one side of the gym. Delia's dad and Jillian sat on the other. Misty's mother and her four little sisters waved proudly from a seat near the door.

"Look, Delia! It's Miss Benson!" Yolanda said with excitement. Both girls waved furiously to their teacher as she walked into the gym. She waved back, finding a seat near several of her students.

Yolanda waved to her parents as well, then asked Randy, "Is your dad coming? I know he never misses a big tournament if he's in town."

Randy replied, "No, he's still in California, but he told

me to tell you to jump pretty and kick butt!" Delia glanced at Randy, but said nothing.

The president of the American Double Dutch League, who always showed up dressed in a classy hat, welcomed each team. After singing the national anthem in several languages, representing each country there, she led the jumpers in the recitation of the Double Dutch Pledge.

Delia repeated loud and strong with the voices of six hundred other jumpers:

> "I promise to do my best to:
> • report for practice on time;
> • work cooperatively with my coach, team-
>   mates, and Double Dutch officials;
> • strive to encourage good citizenship,
>   always setting a good example;
> • practice good health habits—promising to
>   be drug free;
> • demonstrate my best with daily school
>   attendance, assignments, and home
>   responsibilities."

It was time. The trophies sat ready on a table at the far end of the gym—gleaming and ready for the winners. The buzzers sounded, and the competition began.

twenty-one

"THE FEELING IS DIFFERENT TODAY," DELIA TOLD RANDY, who was handing out water bottles to the girls. "It's like electricity—it will give you a buzz if you touch it. That's how the air feels."

"You're just nervous," Randy replied. "Relax. Concentrate. You can do this."

"I know. We're ready," Delia said, then she joined Yolanda, Charlene, and Misty, who were stretching on the sidelines while the first set of jumpers began. All five of the qualifying third-grade singles teams were on the floor at one time, with several judges, dressed all in white, stationed at each position.

"This is gonna move so fast today," Misty commented. "With five going at a time, they'll be ready for us before we have a chance to go to the bathroom."

"I'm never going to the bathroom away from home again!" Yolanda joked.

The director of the tournament, with the excitement and power of an announcer for the Olympics, roared into the microphone, "Turners, check your ropes! Jumpers, check your laces. Judges, check your timers!" He paused for effect. The gym, filled with hundreds of people, was absolutely silent. "Jumpers, are you ready?" Five very small hands were raised to indicate they were ready to begin. "Judges, are you ready?" Five more hands were raised. "TIME!"

The buzzer sounded, shattering the silence as the third-grade girls began their compulsories.

"Their voices are so tiny," Delia whispered to Yolanda as the third graders chanted the rhythm of the routine.

"Yeah, but they're good for being so young. They've been jumping less than a year."

"Not one miss—they're dynamite!"

When the buzzer sounded and the third graders scrambled off the floor to be replaced by the fourth graders, Delia and the others grabbed them and hugged them fiercely. Bomani's grin was massive. "Big smiles—big hearts. That's what I like. Good job, Little Bees," Bomani told them as they sipped their water bottles and waited like professionals for the next round.

The competition progressed quickly. When the eighth-grade teams singles were called, Randy yelled to Delia, Yolanda, and Charlene, "Remember what my daddy said— jump pretty and kick butt!" Misty gave the three of them a hug and whispered a quick word of encouragement. They smiled and waved to Randy, but when they got to their positions on the gym floor, their faces turned stony, tight with concentration, as they waited for the signal to begin.

They jumped smoothly for their singles routine, but Delia missed twice during the speed jumps. Each time she missed, she could hear the crowd sigh, "Oh!" as she scrambled to get back in the ropes and regain her momentum. Even with the two misses, however, she managed to jump a 340. She left the floor, a little out of breath, feeling proud nevertheless.

"Good job, Delia," Randy said with a grin. She smiled back and sat with relief on the hard bleacher bench.

"What did the other eighth-grade teams look like?" Yolanda asked Misty.

"One team really messed up—the girl missed during her speed jumps about seven times. I felt sorry for her," Misty replied. "The rest of them were really good—and the team from South Carolina made no misses at all, but she jumped a lot slower than you. You get bonus points for speed, so I think you three are still in the running."

As they sipped their water, Yolanda whispered, "Did you see them?"

"Who?" asked Delia, glancing around.

"The Tollivers!" Yolanda said with excitement. "They're in the stands—sitting in the top row of the bleachers, way in the corner at the far end of the gym."

Delia looked up in amazement, and there they sat—unsmiling as usual, sitting together, watching the rhythmic frenzy on the floor below. "You got the power, girl," Delia told Yolanda. "What are you gonna do now?"

"I don't know," Yolanda said, giggling. "I'm thinking about asking them to be my personal bodyguards. What do you think?"

"I think you're trippin'!" Delia laughed.

By the time Delia, Misty, Charlene, and Yolanda were called for their doubles freestyle routine, the tension in the gym seemed to be even tighter. The results for the entire tournament would be announced in less than an hour. They took a deep breath, picked up the ropes, and the buzzer blared loudly once more. Freestyle competitions were judged singly, so all eyes were on them as they began the complicated routine.

Delia and Misty did leap-frog jumps over the heads of Charlene and Yolanda, who turned the ropes wide and low so they could complete the complicated trick without getting tangled up. They moved then to a wheelbarrow, where Misty jumped on her hands while Delia held her feet. Another jumping twist and Yolanda flipped into a bouncing back flip and handed her end of the ropes to Misty. Delia grabbed the other end of the ropes, so that Charlene and Yolanda now jumped in the center where the other two girls had jumped just seconds before. The four girls worked in unison—two turners and two jumpers—while the ropes continued to twirl, then Charlene did a reverse turn and managed to make it look like a karate kick. They finished with several high can-can jumps, tossed the ropes deftly to one side, and landed in splits together in front of the judges' table, their heads resting on their crisscrossed arms. The audience exploded in cheers; they recognized a good routine when they saw one.

Delia, Charlene, Misty, and Yolanda took one last bow and bounded off the floor, breathless with excitement and success. All of their team members ran to hug them, from the youngest to the oldest—that routine had made them *all* look good.

"Awesome!" Randy roared as he gave the four of them a huge hug. "You did it!"

Delia grinned with pride. *It doesn't get any better than this,* she thought. Even though they were sitting on opposite sides of the gym, her parents were in the stands, cheering for her. Her friends were close by, helping them win today. And there were no worries about stupid school stuff, like reading or tests, for weeks, at least. And maybe they'd go home from here with big, fat trophies and red champion jackets.

Then she glanced at Randy and sighed. She felt so bad for him. Right now he didn't have anybody except for his Double Dutch friends and Bomani. What would happen if the police caught his father? What if Randy had to move away? Was that why he'd told her he was moving to California? He was better than a boyfriend—he was a good friend—and she would really miss having him around.

Then she felt Yolanda poke her in the side. "That team was awesome!" she said, pointing to the girls leaving the floor. Delia forced her concentration back to the tournament.

She and her teammates watched the last few freestyle routines, then there was nothing to do but wait while the judges tallied the scores. They huddled over computers and conferred with one another in little groups, while the teams sat nervously in the stands. Kids in matching T-shirts walked quietly together around the gym, too tense to sit down. A three-year-old casually pushed his own stroller across the gym floor, while his five-year-old sister pretended to jump the way she'd seen the teams do all day. Very few people left the gym, which was hot and stuffy by now, filled to capacity with sweat and dreams and nervous anticipation.

"Ladies and gentlemen! We are proud to announce the winners of this year's World Invitational Championship of the American Double Dutch League," the announcer began. "Would the five finalist third-grade teams please come to the floor!"

Cincinnati's Little Bees hurried to the floor. They joined

hands with the members of the other teams, all of them waiting in anticipation so intense, they could not stand still. They wiggled and shifted their feet and waited in silent expectation. "In fifth place," the booming voice announced, "are the Beanie Babies from California! Congratulations!" The Beanie Babies, looking a little disappointed at being selected fifth place, walked to the table to receive their small trophies.

"Let's give these young ladies a special round of applause!" the announcer reminded his audience. "They have been jumping for only a few months, and already they have reached championship level! For everyone who competed today is a champion!" The audience cheered loudly, knowing that building self-esteem was as important as winning. The little girls held their heads a bit higher as they marched off the floor clutching their trophies. Cincinnati's Little Bees took a respectable second place, and they ran off the floor with their trophies, feeling very proud of themselves.

When the results of the eighth-grade singles teams were announced, Delia, Yolanda, and Charlene also took second place.

"This is good," Delia told Charlene as she glanced at the trophy.

"Yeah, really good—almost excellent," Charlene agreed. Both girls sighed.

"We wanted first place, didn't we?" Yolanda said honestly.

"Yeah, but we're proud of what we've done, aren't we?" asked Delia.

"Yeah, really proud," Charlene and Yolanda answered together. But their voices were quiet and subdued.

double dutch

By the time the announcer got to the doubles teams, eighth-grade level, Delia's hands were clammy with nervous excitement. The Cincinnati fourth- and fifth-grade singles team had each taken a first place. The rest of the Cincinnati teams had taken seconds and thirds.

"I *really* want one of those bright red champion jackets with the words 'Double Dutch World Champion' on the back!" Delia whispered to Yolanda as they took their place near the table of trophies, waiting for the director to announce the results of the eighth-grade doubles competition.

"Yeah—me, too. I look good in red!" Yolanda whispered back.

They joined hands and listened while the fifth-place team was called. They sighed with relief as those girls moved out of line. The four remaining teams rejoined hands and waited for the next announcement. The director called the fourth- and third-place teams, each receiving an increasingly larger trophy. Only two teams remained.

Delia was finding it hard to breathe. The announcer paused for effect because whenever the second-place team was called, the other team knew it was automatically the first-place champion. "The second-place team is . . . the Rocketeers from Virginia!" The Rocketeers moved to receive their awards with a mixture of pride and disappointment, while Yolanda, Charlene, Misty, and Delia hugged and jumped in place, screaming with excitement. "And now, ladies and gentleman, may I introduce the world champion eighth-grade doubles team—the Queen Bees of Cincinnati, Ohio!" Every single Ohio jumper, and most of the people in the huge audience, stood and whooped with delight, some of them holding their own trophies or clutching the coveted red jackets. Delia could see her mother jumping in the stands like a teenager. Charlene's grandmother stood stiffly but proudly as she waved to the girls. Misty's younger sisters looked like little jumping beans. Yolanda's mother looked like she was crying. Even Yolanda's dad looked pleased.

Delia, Yolanda, Misty, and Charlene bounded to the table, almost too excited to stand still long enough to have the red jackets placed on their shoulders and the huge golden trophies placed in their shaking hands. Cameras flashed, pictures were taken, and they were suddenly back on the bleachers, a giggling, bubbling group of winners. Bomani snapped pictures like crazy—he took photos of the trophy, the jackets, the girls, the rest of the team, Randy, and even a close-up of himself grinning into the lens of the camera. He couldn't stop hooting and cheering.

Randy touched the soft satin of Delia's red jacket and the incredibly golden shine of the huge trophy. "Awesome!" he whispered.

"You deserve a trophy, too, Randy," Delia said with feeling. "We wouldn't be able to do what we do without you and Bomani."

"Yeah, I know," Randy answered with a grin. "Just as long as you appreciate me!"

The director of the tournament announced the rest of the results over the next few minutes, with excited, triumphant kids accepting their acclaim. In an unofficial parade of champions, Delia and her team and a few other red-jacketed girls marched around the gym, waving to the crowd and wearing those red jackets in spite of the heat.

Delia even waved to the Tolliver brothers, who, to her surprise, waved back.

As the gym gradually cleared of exhausted jumpers and observers, Delia noticed Yolanda talking quietly to the Tollivers, who quickly disappeared into the crowd as her parents walked over to give her hugs and congratulations. Delia's dad and Jillian had hugged her and left quickly, a procedure they usually followed at events like this so that her mother would not feel so stressed. Delia appreciated that. She knew her mom would be waiting in the car.

Randy checked the bleachers for empty water bottles and potato chip wrappers, making sure their area of the gym was clean. Delia joined him, silently tossing trash into the can and picking up forgotten items.

"Look what I found," she said. "A watch, a book, and a Barbie doll—these third graders crack me up."

Randy said nothing. He was sitting on the top bleacher, looking stunned, an unfolded sheet of paper in his hands. Delia recognized it immediately.

"This fell out of your gym bag," he said quietly. "I thought I was doing you a favor by picking up your stuff, and look what I find," he continued, trying to explain away the confusion on his face. "Why did you hide this from me? I gotta find a phone and call this number right away!" He jumped up and started down the bleachers, smoky anger covering his face.

Delia's heart beat faster. "Wait, Randy! Don't call yet! Let me explain."

Randy glared at her. "I don't want to hear nothin' from you! Where you get off messin' in my life?" He bounded down the bleachers, two at a time.

twenty-two

RANDY, CLUTCHING THE FLYER DELIA HAD FOUND, RAN across the gym and headed to the pay phone in the corner. Delia knew it was out of order, because she had tried to use it earlier that day, but she was afraid to say anything else to Randy. She had never seen him so angry. She watched with dismay as he slammed the phone to the floor.

Bomani came back into the gym then, and Randy ran to him, talking quickly and rattling the flyer in this hand. Delia couldn't hear the conversation, but she figured that Randy was telling Bomani what a low-life friend she turned out to be. Bomani glanced at her, and she lowered her head in shame. He carefully read the sheet of paper, then spoke quietly to Randy, who seemed to calm down. Delia was afraid to move as she saw Randy walk back over to where she sat. He did not smile.

"I gotta go. Bomani said I should call the number on the flyer from his house, 'cause its long distance." He turned and headed toward the door.

Delia was near tears. "I'm sorry, Randy. I didn't want to upset you. I was going to tell you after the tournament that I found that flyer. I knew you'd be upset to know that criminal posters about your dad were hanging around. It's got to be embarrassing for you to know your dad is wanted by the police."

Randy turned suddenly. "Criminal?" Randy roared. "Are you crazy? My father is no criminal!"

Delia jumped back a little from the power and anger of Randy's reply. "What do you mean?" she asked in confusion. "The poster . . . the police . . ." She hesitated.

"This is the first clue I've had in months," Randy explained. "My first real hope."

"Randy, I don't understand," Delia admitted. Her brain felt fuzzy. "I thought you said your dad wanted you to move to California?"

Randy took a deep breath. "I guess I should have told you the truth. My dad has been missing for the last two months."

"What do you mean 'missing'? You told me you talk to him all the time."

"I didn't want anybody to find out, so I've been covering for him. Every day I figured he'd come back. But he didn't. I haven't heard from him since he left on a long-distance haul."

"Oh, Randy, you've been all by yourself?" Delia gasped.

"That's why I've been so hungry all the time, and so hard up for cash."

"Why didn't you tell me?"

"I thought he'd deserted me, like my mother did," Randy replied quietly. "But this flyer tells me different and you hid it from me!" Randy's anger was returning.

"So what does the poster say?" Delia asked hesitantly. "He's not wanted by the police?"

"Can't you read, Delia?" Randy asked, looking at her as if she were one of Yolanda's Martians.

Delia sat on the bleacher and finally released the torment of the last few years. She cried loud and long, ignoring the stares of the few remaining people in the gym. "No, Randy," she said finally. "I can't read. I've been faking it for years." She repeated for emphasis, and the words seemed to echo in the almost deserted gym: "I do not know how to read."

"How is that possible? Everybody knows how to read!" Randy answered in disbelief.

"It's easy if you know how to play the game. At the store when I shop for groceries for my mom, I know the colors and the sizes of the packages I want. At the fast-food places they have pictures of everything. I just ask for a number two with a Coke. At school, I guess, I listen real good, I get the video instead of reading the book, and I do really well on nonreading reports like our project for English. But it's hard to keep up," she admitted. "I'm so tired of it all."

"What does your mother say about your, uh, reading problem, Delia?"

"She doesn't know," Delia replied. She pulled at the hair of the Barbie doll.

"That's impossible. How can a mother NOT know something like that?"

"It's not so hard to hide the truth, Randy. Look at what you did. Nobody knew you were living all alone."

Randy sighed. "I guess you're right."

"I feel so stupid," Delia said with her head down.

"But you seem so smart!" Randy blurted out. "I'm sorry, I didn't mean to say you were dumb."

"I wasn't smart enough to read that flyer about your

father," Delia said quietly. "I really AM stupid. What does it say?"

"The police aren't looking for him—they have *found* him!" Randy said with excitement.

"What? How? Where is he? He's . . . alive?" she asked cautiously.

"Yeah, at least he was when this flyer was made up. There's no telling how old it is. Looks like it was sent out as a fax from a hospital in Columbus, Ohio. Gee, Dad," Randy mused, "you only got as far as Columbus?" He shook his head in disbelief.

"Wasn't he on his way to California?" Delia asked.

"Yeah, he was. From what I can tell here, he was beat up and robbed and left for dead near a truck stop. How'd you let them get the drop on you like that, Dad?" Randy said more to himself than to Delia. "He was in a coma for six weeks, but it seems, now that he has come out of it, his memory is foggy, and they are looking for anyone who knows him and can help him. And that's me!" It was Randy's turn to break down with emotion. "I was afraid he was dead, Delia."

"I almost threw that flyer away, Randy. I thought it was something really bad that would hurt you. Because I'm so stupid, I almost cost you the chance to get your daddy back."

Randy didn't disagree with her. Instead, he said, "I gotta go. I gotta make this call." Clutching the flyer, he ran out suddenly, leaving Delia sitting alone on the bleachers, listening to the echoes of all the victories and defeats that gym had witnessed—including her own.

twenty-three

M RS. D OUGLAS WALKED INTO THE GYM, LOOKING FOR Delia. "You ready to go?" she asked. "I was so proud of you today, Delia—jumping on that floor like there was no tomorrow."

Delia thought, *I guess she's right—there IS no tomorrow. I'm dumb as a rock and I always will be!* To her mother she said with a smile, "Thanks, Mom."

"What's wrong, honey?" her mother asked as she gathered up the second-place trophy and the huge first-place trophy.

"Just tired, Mom," Delia replied. "It's been a long day."

"I have an idea," her mother suggested. "Let's go out to dinner to celebrate—someplace really nice."

"I'd like that, Mom," Delia said quietly. They walked slowly out of the silent gym and into the early evening, the last bit of sun splashing off the gold of Delia's trophies. Delia, quiet and thoughtful during the ride to the restaurant, was thankful her mother didn't pepper her with questions and meaningless mother-talk.

The restaurant was cool and lit with candles flickering on each table. Delia slid into the well-stuffed, comfortable seat and sighed with a bit of relief. The waiter brought two menus, glasses of water, and bread sticks, then hovered closely for their order.

"Give us a minute to look this over, would you?" Mrs. Douglas said to him.

"No problem, ma'am." The waiter disappeared into the shadows.

Delia looked at the menu and froze. It had no pictures on it like the menus in the restaurants that she and her friends usually visited. She held it tightly in front of her and tried to focus on the words. She squinted. She held it close to her eyes, then far away. Nothing helped. The words did their usual dance of disobedience.

"Where are your glasses?" her mother asked, noticing Delia's difficulty.

"I didn't bring them. I didn't think I'd need them today since all we were doing is jumping. I just use them for reading."

"Do they help?" her mother asked.

"Not really," Delia mumbled.

"Do you think we need to get the prescription adjusted? It's been a couple of years since you've seen the eye doctor."

"Yeah, probably," Delia replied. She nibbled on a bread stick. She decided she'd just order a hamburger and fries, like she always did. That way, she wouldn't have to worry about what the menu says. But she was so sick of hamburgers! Some pasta or some steak or some chicken would be great. But she couldn't figure out enough on the complicated menu to tell which was which. Delia sighed again.

"Are you ready to order?" The waiter had reappeared from the shadows.

"I'll have a hamburger and fries, please," Delia said with resignation.

"Tonight is a celebration, Delia—for you," her mother said. "Don't you want to order something different tonight?"

Delia hesitated. Then she sighed and said, "Thanks, Mom, but I really like hamburgers."

Mrs. Douglas ordered shrimp and pasta, and Delia wished she had as well. She slumped further into her seat. Her mother smiled and said, "Cheer up, Delia! You've lived through a tornado! You're a champion! You've got more trophies than we can fit on our mantel! Why are you looking like you just lost your best friend?"

"I think maybe I did," Delia replied.

"Yolanda? She looked great out there, although I admit I was a little worried about her—jumping like that so soon after what could have been a really serious injury."

"No, not Yo Yo," Delia said quietly. "Randy."

"Oh, no wonder you look so glum," her mother answered in that mother-knows-all tone of voice. "Did you and he have a fight?"

"Not really, I did something really stupid and it . . . never mind, here comes the food." The waiter effortlessly whipped the food in front of them and retreated after refilling their water glasses.

"You want to tell me about it?" Mrs. Douglas asked as she dipped her shrimp in the butter sauce.

Delia glanced at her hamburger, which was dry and overcooked, and looked with longing at her mother's plate. "I wish I had ordered the pasta," Delia said, sniffing the garlic flavor that drifted from her mother's plate.

"You had your chance—it's delicious," Mrs. Douglas replied. "But what does that have to do with you and the problem with Randy?"

"Nothing. Everything." Delia tried to blink back the tears. "You know, Mom, they'll fix the school building eventually or make us take classes someplace else, and they'll make us take that test eventually, too."

"Of course they will, dear," her mother replied. "Not even tornadoes can stop the school process for very long. But what's wrong?"

"Mom," Delia whispered, her voice barely louder than the flicker of the candle in front of them. "I can't read. This is not one of Yolanda's tall tales—this is for real. I can't read my books at school. I can't read the newspaper. I didn't order the shrimp because I couldn't read the stupid menu."

Mrs. Douglas dropped her fork. She tried to speak, but nothing came out of her mouth.

"I've been hiding it, Mom, and I'm tired of pretending. I almost cost Randy his father because of it. You have to believe me. You gotta find me some help so the words quit jumping on the page like they're jumping Double Dutch." Delia's eyes, rimmed with tears, looked directly into the amazed eyes of her mother. "I can't read, Mom."

Delia's mother stared at her daughter, disbelief on her face. Delia sensed her thinking back through years of mystery about irregular grades and peculiar study habits. After a long moment, she said, "I believe you. Oh, my Lord, so much makes sense now! Delia, why didn't you say something sooner?"

"What was I supposed to say? 'Hey, Mom, guess what? I'm a dummy!'" Delia replied, sniffing, as she told her mother about how she had slipped around the edges of reading for so long.

"Now I *know* you are intelligent. To be able to fake it this long shows amazing ingenuity. We just have to figure out how to open the doors of your brain that are locked right now," her mother said with authority.

"I've got scrambled brains," Delia said as she dipped a cold French fry into her ketchup. "I've never seen anybody unscramble eggs. What makes you think somebody can unscramble my head?"

Her mother laughed softly. "You'd be surprised what modern science and education can do today. Once again, I am very proud of you, Delia. First thing Monday morning we're going to get you evaluated and get to the bottom of this. We'll get you a tutor, a doctor, whatever it takes. Maybe even a specialist—your dad will help pay for it!" she said sharply.

"I'm a loser," Delia mumbled, her head bent so low over her plate she could see the texture of the hamburger bun.

"Let me tell you something, Delia," her mother began. "I'm the one who feels like a failure here. I remember when you were about two, I took you to the shoe store to get new shoes. I had just bought you shoes maybe two months before that, but the saleslady looked at me like I was some kind of abusive parent, telling me, 'Your child's foot is *severely* constricted in this shoe. Didn't you notice that she had outgrown her current shoe?' I felt so bad because it just hadn't occurred to me that your foot would grow so fast. I didn't *mean* to be a bad mother, but I guess I was. So that's how I feel now—I should have noticed you were struggling. That's a mother's job."

Delia looked at her mother in surprise. "You had your own problems to deal with—all that mess with Daddy. Everybody else learns to read with no help at all. I was just too dumb to do that."

"Quit talking bad about yourself! You jumped like a winner today, because that's what you are," Mrs. Douglas said fiercely. "Losers don't get to wear that beautiful jacket you've got on."

"I didn't have to read to win it," Delia countered.

"But you had to work hard. You are a champion, inside and out, and champions know it takes hard work to succeed. This may not get fixed overnight, you know. But we'll get there—you and me together."

"I know," Delia replied with relief, glad the problem was now in her mother's hands. "And Mom?"

"What, Delia? Is there more?"

Delia smiled. "Can I have the rest of your pasta? I'm really sick of hamburgers!" They both laughed, the awful tension of the evening flickering away like the candle that the waiter extinguished as he brought the bill.

twenty-four

DELIA TOOK A LONG SHOWER WHEN THEY GOT HOME, THEN headed for the phone. She had to find out about Randy and his father. But before she could pick it up to dial, it shrilled loudly as her hand touched the receiver. It was Yolanda.

"What's up, my red-jacketed girlfriend?" Yolanda said cheerfully.

"Not much. Me and my mom went out to eat after the tournament. We had one of those mother-daughter talks."

"She finally got around to talking about sex?" Yolanda laughed.

Delia chuckled. "No, probably by the time I'm twenty-five she'll get the nerve to do that!"

"Parents are so backward," Yolanda agreed. "When I was five, I had to sit my mother down and tell *her* about sex!" She was laughing so hard, it sounded as if she had dropped the phone. "Seriously, what did you talk about?"

"I told her about my problems at school—my broken brain. You're right about parents being backward. It's amazing she never figured it out. I dumped it all on her."

"How'd she take it? What'd she say?" asked Yo Yo.

"I think she felt bad, like she was a bad parent or something. But basically she was pretty cool."

174

"I am *so* glad that's out of the box. Lies will get you nowhere," Yolanda said mischievously.

Delia laughed. "Look who's talking—the teen queen of extreme!" Trying to change the subject, she asked Yolanda, "So, how's it going with your double dudes?"

"Two is better than one, I guess. Believe it or not, they're really shy, but they're very good at acting mean."

"They fooled me," Delia said, shuddering as she remembered.

"Let's put it this way—we won't be going on any double dates anytime soon. They're not ready for Yolanda's fast track yet!"

Delia chuckled and looked at the clock. "Hey, I gotta call Randy before it gets too late. I'll catch you tomorrow, Yo Yo. Bye."

Delia called Bomani's house, but the answering machine picked up, so she dialed Randy's number, not really expecting an answer. She was surprised when she heard his deep bass voice. "Randy! I didn't really expect you to be there. What's going on?"

Randy didn't sound glad to hear from Delia. She knew he still had to be very angry. "I came to get a few clothes and my cat. Bomani says she can stay in his garage as long as I'm staying there with him." He said nothing else.

Delia hesitated. "Did you call the phone number on the flyer?"

"Yeah," Randy replied.

She could hear him breathing slowly on the other end. "What did they say?" she whispered.

"It's my dad, for sure," Randy answered with feeling. "I

described the mole on his nose and the tattoo on his left arm that he got in the army."

"Did they give you any information about him? Like what happened? Is he gonna be okay?"

Randy's voice sounded choked. "From what I can figure out, his truck was found abandoned in Texas but from what they can piece together, he never even got out of Ohio. He was beat up by more than one person, the doctor told me. Knowing Dad, he probably picked up some hitchhikers again. He trusts everybody."

"Go on," Delia prodded. "What else did they tell you?"

"They took all his identification, his cell phone, his money—as well as his truck—and left him for dead after beating him in the head with a hammer."

Delia shuddered. "Oh, no! Your poor dad! Randy, I'm so sorry you have to go through this."

"Some lady on vacation from Canada found him and called the police, but they had no way of knowing who he was. He was almost dead. The doctor said he just started coming out of it a few days ago—around the time of the tornado. They sent flyers out by fax to places within a hundred miles of Columbus to see if anybody recognized him."

"Well, I'm glad I recognized the picture, at least. If it had been all words, I would never have known," Delia told him with real remorse.

"Well, I'm glad you can read pictures," Randy said tersely.

Delia could hear the anger in his voice. She asked quietly, "Is he going to recover?"

"I think so. The doctor said he's talking a little now, about trucks and cats."

"That's good!" Delia said, trying to sound cheerful. "Are you going to go see him soon? Is Bomani going to take you? Maybe me and my mom could drive you up to Columbus," she offered. "It's the least I can do—I feel like some of this is my fault."

"No!" Randy replied loudly. "Bomani's gonna take me up there in the morning. I gotta go, Delia." He hung up without saying good-bye.

Delia stared into the phone for a moment, feeling empty and lost.

twenty-five

THE NEXT MORNING, AS RANDY CLIMBED INTO BOMANI'S van, he asked, "Hey, Bomani? Do you mind if we make one stop before we head to Columbus? I gotta see a friend. It will only take a minute."

"Sure, Randy. No problem," Bomani replied easily. Randy gave directions, and as soon as the van stopped, Randy bounded out of the door and into the pawn shop.

"Hey, Mr. Clifford! Remember me?" Randy called out as he entered the dimly lit store.

Mr. Clifford, who Randy was sure had on the same gray sweater he'd had on when he had first met him, ambled slowly from the back of the store. *It's probably the same cigar stuck in the corner of his mouth,* Randy thought, chuckling. Mr. Clifford, purple-rimmed glasses on his nose, smiled broadly when he saw Randy. "Ah, Mr. Youngblood," he said. "You have more valuables to offer me?"

"No, man. I, uh, I just wanted to let you know my dad is gonna be okay. And I wanted to, you know, uh, thank you. You kept me from drowning. If you want me to help you out around here after school or something, I can do that now—at least when my dad is back to work." Randy looked at the floor.

"Stop by anytime, Youngblood."

Randy grinned, yelled his thanks once more, and bounded out of the door and back to Bomani's van, thanking him for stopping.

"What was that all about?" Bomani asked.

"Just an old friend," Randy said quietly. "He helped me when I was down." He said nothing more, but sank into the seat and gazed out the window.

"What about your other friends—like Delia?" Bomani asked as they drove through the Sunday morning traffic on I-71.

"What about her?" Randy replied gruffly.

"I heard you hang up on her yesterday," Bomani told him. "I bet she's feeling pretty bad about all this."

"Tough!" Randy felt his anger returning.

Bomani said nothing else for several miles.

"If I hadn't found that piece of paper, Delia might have thrown it away. I might have been alone forever!"

"But you did, and she didn't, and you won't. So give the kid a break," Bomani suggested.

This time, Randy was silent for several miles. He thought about Delia as he watched the rural countryside whiz by. And he thought about his father.

"I'm scared," Randy said finally. "Maybe my dad won't recognize me. Maybe it will never be like it used to be between us."

"Everything changes, Randy, and yet somehow things remain constant. Every year I have a different group of kids in Double Dutch, with different needs and problems, but somehow, everything manages to stay the same, except I think I'm getting older!" Bomani chuckled.

They rode the rest of the way in thoughtful silence.

twenty-six

LATE SUNDAY AFTERNOON DELIA SAT ON THE FRONT STEPS of her house, wishing she had a large, wraparound porch like the houses she had seen on TV, but she and her mom had only three front steps and a small landing that barely left enough room for a chair. Delia, wearing her red jacket, and a pair of blue jeans that were fresh from the dryer, sat in a kitchen chair that she had dragged outside so she could enjoy the soft spring breezes. It was a day of beauty—the kind of day you read about in books, she thought. As she watched the high, thin clouds brush across the sky, it seemed as if the storms of the last week were a memory of the distant past.

But she had plenty of new storms to deal with. Her mother was inside on the phone, having another argument with her father—this time about whose fault it was that Delia had a reading problem.

She had resigned herself to the reality that she had to face that state test eventually, and she knew that she'd probably have to take it several times before she conquered it. But as she touched the bright red silkiness of her jacket, she was determined to do it.

Yo Yo had called earlier, rattling on about the Tollivers and Jesse, who didn't like the idea that the Tollivers had been calling her. She loved it. Delia didn't tell Yolanda, but she envied her. Yo Yo breezed through school and collected boyfriends along the way.

Delia looked up at one small dark cloud in the bright sky and thought of Randy. The loss of his friendship hurt more than listening to her parents fight. Angry at herself for not being able to read, and feeling stupid as well, she hated the fact that her problems had caused Randy pain. Delia wondered how the visit went with Randy's father.

Her mother came to the door then. Delia could tell she had been crying. "I'm sorry, Mom," Delia said.

"No, sweetheart, I'm the one who's sorry. We're going to work this out, I promise."

"I know, Mom. It's not your fault. I'm gonna try real hard." Delia wanted to change the subject. "Are you off the phone? I want to call Bomani."

"Oh, my goodness! I almost forgot. Randy's on the phone. I'm so glad he called—it gave me a reason to get off the line with your father. I'll bring the phone out here."

Delia's heart pounded as her mother handed her the phone. "Hi, Randy," she said softly.

"What's up?" he replied.

Delia thought he sounded really subdued. "Did you see your dad?"

"Yeah, we just got back. Oh, Delia, he's gonna be fine. He looked like a little skinny, older, slightly beat-up version of himself, but he almost jumped out of his bed when he saw me. His whole face was a big ol' grin!"

"I'm so glad, Randy. Will he be able to come home soon?"

"Yeah, the doctor said my visit made a big difference, so my dad can probably come home in just a few days."

"That's real good news, Randy," Delia said with feeling. "I am so glad."

"I guess I'd better clean up the house a little before he gets here. I'm so excited!"

"Randy, I've been thinking about you all day," Delia admitted. "I'm so sorry—about everything." She giggled a little. "Actually I just had this same conversation with my mother!"

"It's not your fault, Delia. Actually, if it hadn't been for you, and for that Double Dutch tournament, I never would have seen that flyer."

"Well, I still feel pretty stupid. By the way, me and my mom had a long talk. I told her everything. Monday she's taking me to some learning center to get tested, and maybe in a hundred years I can actually pass a test!" She lowered her voice. "It's a little embarrassing."

"It won't take that long, Delia," Randy said. "You wear that red championship jacket when you go and they will know they're dealing with a winner!"

"Thanks—and Randy?"

"Yeah?"

"I'm glad you're back."

"Me, too."

Delia's eyes stung with tears as she hung up the phone. She wiped her eyes, then sat quietly on her little porch, trying to make sense of everything—Double Dutch, the tornado, the Tollivers, Randy and his dad, and all the secrets that had almost destroyed several lives. Delia listened to the cars as they whizzed by. The movement of the cars on the street, the clouds scudding across the sky, and even the beating of her heart made her think of the sounds and rhythms of the ropes when she jumped. She smiled and headed back into the house, carrying the rhythms with her.

Double Dutch

Delia loves Double Dutch jump roping. And she's good at it. *Really* good. But Delia is using her success to mask an embarrassing secret: She doesn't know how to read. Her friend Randy has a secret too. His dad has been missing for weeks and he's almost out of money, but he's afraid to ask for help.

These two storylines collide at the World Double Dutch Championship as Delia and Randy are also forced to deal with the very real threat of violence at school, coming from two of their fellow students, the menacing Tolliver twins, who also have a secret: They like to make people scared. But will they act on their threats?

Discussion Topics

Double Dutch begins with a discussion of the characters' fear of the Tolliver twins. Trace how the idea of fear and the results of fear are developed throughout the story.

The twins use intimidation and fear to terrorize the school. Analyze the names Titan and Tabu. Why are their names intimidating? What other factors about the twins make them seem dangerous and deadly?

Why is the television program, which the twins appear on, an effective way to increase their negative reputation? Discuss the effect of these kinds of talk shows.

Yolanda is a humorous character because she tells tall tales and exaggerates. Basically, however, she is a liar. Discuss, by using other characters in the story, how lies and deception can have serious consequences. How can the character of Yolanda be justified if lying is a negative trait?

Many of the characters are hiding secrets. Tell how the characters listed below have secrets that they are hiding from others and explain how those secrets caused problems:

- **Titan and Tabu**   • **Delia**   • **Randy**
- **Yolanda**   • **Delia's parents**

Double Dutch is more than just a story about jumping rope. Discuss how the title can have more than one interpretation. Find all examples of "double" ideas and events in the story.

The tornado is a natural disaster that brings about a number of plot developments. Explain how the tornado can be interpreted as a "character" that affects the rest of the characters and events in the book.

Families often have difficulties and young people must cope with the situations that arise. Discuss the relationship between the following characters and the strengths of their families:

- **Delia and her mother**
- **Delia and her father**
- **Randy and his father**
- **Bomani and his family**

A powerful friendship can often make a difference in the lives of young people. Discuss how Delia's friendships with Yolanda and Randy make a difference in her life. What might have happened if Yolanda and Randy had not been real friends to Delia?

Delia's problem is that she cannot read, yet she is obviously very intelligent. Give examples of Delia's intelligence and show how she was able to escape detection for so long.

Double Dutch is a popular team sport. Discuss how organized sports and athletic events are positive activities. Trace how the sport of double Dutch was helpful in the lives of the following characters:

- **Delia**
- **Randy**
- **Misty**
- **Yolanda**

Minor characters are often very important in the development of a story. Discuss how the following characters made a difference:

- **Mr. Clifford**
- **Bomani**
- **Miss Benson**
- **Mrs. Parks**

What predictions can you make about the following?

- **Delia and the test**
- **Delia and Double Dutch**
- **Delia and Randy**
- **Tabu and Titan at school**
- **Yolanda and the twins**
- **Randy and his father**

Writing Activities

Comparison Paper

"Sometimes it's hard to tell the difference between the truth and a lie," Delia mused. "And it doesn't really matter who believes it."

Write a comparison paper on the difference between truths and lies, on the difference between what is real and what is believed. Use examples from the book to support your statements.

Descriptive Paper

"The tension in the small gym sizzled like dangling electric lines—hot and fiery."

"Soon nothing could be heard but the tapping of her shoes and the whirling of the ropes as they made a breeze in the corner of the gym."

"It was the test. It was rumbling down the road like a runaway truck, and she was standing helplessly directly in its path."

"He thought about real fear and how it was slipping like smoke under his door, into his space, and throughout his body."

Write a descriptive paper using one of the four sentences above, or choose another sentence from the book, as a starter. Use vivid verbs and powerful adjectives and adverbs as you write. Use as many of the senses as you can (sight, sound, smell, touch, and taste).

Narrative Paper

"Clutching the flyer, he ran out suddenly, leaving Delia sitting alone on the bleachers, listening to the echoes of all the victories and defeats that gym witnessed—including her own."

Write a narrative paper from the point of view of the gym. Tell what kinds of games were played, the kind of people that sat there and watched them, the athletes that played, the food that was sold, etc. Take any aspect of "the life of the gym" and develop it.

Expository (Explanatory) Paper

"Double Dutch requires an intricate display of skill, agility, and strength. It encourages creativity, teamwork, and sportsmanship, and develops physical fitness and mental discipline."

Write an expository paper on a sport. Tell how the game is played, give some of its rules, and explain why it is successful as an enjoyable physical activity.

Persuasive Paper

"We are instituting some new policies here at school. It is happening all over the country, so don't think you're being picked on, and don't think you're special. First of all, this weekend a metal detector will be installed at the front door."

Write a persuasive paper that argues the following point: "Metal detectors are useful and necessary and should be installed in all schools to insure safety." You may agree or disagree with this statement, but you may only argue one side of the issue.

Literary Paper

Read the novel *Lord of the Flies*. Write a paper that discusses the ideas of fear and violence, as the students did in Miss Benson's class. Compare ideas from *Double Dutch* with ideas from *Lord of the Flies*.

Poetry

Write a poem about one of the following topics:

- Secrets and lies
- Fear of the unknown
- Forever friends
- The joy of the jump
- Storms and destruction
- The dance of divorce

Suggested Investigations

- Investigate more about the sport of double Dutch. Learn the rules and regulations and learn the steps required. Have a double Dutch tournament at your school.

- Investigate tornadoes or hurricanes as storms of destruction. Find out how they are formed, what causes them, and what their effects are upon the people that are involved in such a storm.

- Investigate TV talk shows. How real are the people that appear on the shows, and how are they chosen? Why are such shows popular?

- Investigate reading problems such as dyslexia. What are the causes and cures? What academic difficulties are encountered? How can a student with reading problems be helped?

- Write a paper that investigates the effects of divorce on young people. You may discuss custody arrangements, adjustment, or financial situations. Show the results of the effects of divorce on school, personal, and social situations. You may show both positive and negative results.

Other Activities

- Create a TV show where Randy and his father are reunited.

- Pretend you are a TV reporter at the scene of the tornado.

- Pretend you are a TV reporter at the scene of the double Dutch tournament.

- Create a skit similar to the one that the students produced for class.

- Create a skit that acts out the reunion of the characters in ten years.